THE NORTH COUNTRY CONFESSIONAL

A Novel

CRAIG C. CHARLES

This book is a work of fiction. Names, characters, businesses,
organizations, places, events, and incidents either are the product
of the author's imagination or are used fictitiously. Any
resemblance to actual persons, living or dead, events, or locales is
entirely coincidental.

Library of Congress Catalog Control Number: 2014953376

ISBN 978-0-692-30706-9

Printed in the United States of America

DEDICATION

Writing a book is a selfish act that requires hundreds of hours of isolation. This isolation often comes at the expense of one's family. While I have always put family first, at times I am sure that I have fell short on fulfilling my obligations regarding housework, parenting, and overall engagement with others in order to finish this book. Therefore, I would like to dedicate this creative endeavor to my beautiful and intelligent wife Suzanne and my two amazing children Emma and Alex. I love each of you beyond imagination. Thank you for putting up with me. This book is for you.

ACKNOWLEDGMENTS

Many people had a hand in the development and release of this novel. I would like to thank the following people.

Michelle Josette for her encouragement and professional editing skills.

Clarissa Yeo at YOCLA Designs for her amazing book cover art.

My early readers for their invaluable insights, you know who you are.

To the entire staff at the Mount Washington Hotel, thank you for making me feel at home for over 15 years. You are a haven of relaxation in a fast paced world.

I tell you the past is a bucket of ashes,
— Carl Sandburg

CHAPTER 1

Pickford Marsh looked up at the heavens and scowled, covering his head just as the sky opened up and began to spit on him. He would rather be anywhere but here tonight. Dark water pelted his raincoat as he scurried toward the safety of the hotel's portico. Removing the spattered coat, Pickford reshaped his thinning comb-over which had been victimized by the wind; he started the long descent to The Cave.

The former speakeasy was one of the few places he didn't despise in this ancient relic of a hotel. It reminded him of the medieval dungeons of Europe where tormentors had worked their magic centuries ago. He smiled at the thought, revealing a mouth full of coffee-stained teeth and the stench of rotting flesh. *Just wait*, he thought to himself, *you'll get what you deserve.*

Pickford slithered into the dank room, moving quickly through the iron-gated doorway and into the private back room, near the bar. Taking a seat in one of the darker corners of The

Cave, he blinked his eyes, trying to adjust to the darkness, then he checked his watch. He'd wait just five minutes before leaving.

The end of a cigarette glowed as a figure in the dark just across the table from Pickford began sizing him up. Squinting into the flickering shadows, Pickford searched for something familiar. He saw only a cold blackness that pursued him in his nightmares. He stood up, preparing to leave, when an arm reached out and violently slammed him back down in his chair. Startled by the force, Pickford began to plead, "I don't know who you are, but you've got the wrong —"

"Oh, Iscariot, I'm hurt," teased the voice. "After all we've been through, you don't remember me?"

Pickford's mind raced as he searched the confines of his memory, trying to make sense of the stranger's words. The arm pulled him in closer, threatening him with more violence.

"Perhaps this will jar your memory," the voice hissed, just before planting a deep wet kiss on his lips. "Sit back and listen closely. I'm going to tell you what you're going to do, for something wicked this way returns."

***

The talus deposits at the base of the cliffs should have forewarned me of the dangers lying just ahead, but instinctively I continued to hurtle headlong, straight into the past. The glacier-carved notch was the unofficial southern doorway into the North Country, a stalwart obstacle regulating access to invading flatlanders. I gazed at the scree and wondered if I had made the right decision to return. My thoughts wandered like the snaking road ahead of me while one of my favorite quotes from Katherine Anne Porter weighed heavily on my consciousness.

Although I knew where to physically find Bretton Woods, 'the past is never where you think you left it.'

My driver recounted the history of Franconia Notch as we traversed the mountain pass. A pre-dawn rain had scoured the shear walls, leaving them glistening and flowing with tears disguised as falling cataracts. They wept for me, matching the pain that gnawed inside of me. Unsure what the future held, I knew the answers would be waiting for me in the Great North Woods.

"Are you from the North Country?" the driver asked.

"I was born up here…against my will, but I haven't been back in a long time."

"Well nothing really changes up here so it will probably feel like you never left."

That's what I'm afraid of.

"I've spent my whole life living up here in God's country and I never could think of living anywhere else," the driver added. "You said you're originally from Bretton Woods, did yah?"

"My family was from there."

"Funny, I know just about every brood in Carroll County, but I never heard of the Weeks clan. Is that your father's surname?"

"No, it was my mother's maiden name. She thought it would make things easier for me as a child if I wasn't associated with my father or his family and the expectations that went along with it."

"Did it help yah?"

"Barely," I said, chuckling to myself, "but I escaped as soon as I was old enough to join the Navy."

8

"If you don't mind me asking, what was your father's last name?" the driver pressed on.

I thought about lying or maybe using a more common Québécois surname like Gagnon or Tremblay, but I wanted the driver's pestering questions to end so I told him the truth. "Stickney," I announced while continuing to look out the window.

The car swerved, nearly sideswiping the guardrail and coming dangerously close to propelling us into Echo Lake. The driver regained his composure and command of the limo. He looked at me through the rearview mirror with eyes as wide as the divide between a rich man and a beggar. He couldn't believe I was the one and I couldn't believe I had finally told the truth for the first time in my life.

And so it begins. This is my confession.

***

Emily Baines glanced down at the streets of Midtown Manhattan from her corner office at Tither Publishing and fiddled with the single gray strand of Tahitian pearls that clung around her neck. Rush hour had already paralyzed the streets of the city as throngs of humanity struggled to reach their insignificant evening destinations. *Worker ants*, she told to herself.

She had stayed late, disrupting her normal evening routine of pilates and a massage as she awaited confirmation that the assignment was complete. Her cell phone buzzed, announcing the receipt of the message. A smile blossomed on her face as she read the expected news. The object of her attention had paid the fee just like so many other political malfeasance, celebrities, and religious buskers that Tither had squeezed over the years, avoiding what would have been a very messy and very public scandal. Dirt was her business and business was never better. She verified the $20,000,000 transfer had been processed.

Sitting down, Emily congratulated herself as she poured another glass of Perrier-Jouët and marveled at how far she had come: building Tither Publishing into a media giant with no equal. She rarely thought about the past, but the picture and associated story on the front page of the *New York Times* stopped her cold in her tracks, causing unfamiliar pangs of nostalgia.

"Darby S. Weeks," she said slowly while biting her bottom lip and caressing her pearls. She paced her expansive office for a minute, looking at the picture as memories invaded her mind. Throwing the paper on her desk, she hastily buzzed her personal assistant.

"Olivia, I'm going home to Bretton Woods for a little vacation. Make the necessary arrangements. I want to be in the North Country by tomorrow."

Ready or not, here I come, war hero.

***

The final half hour of the drive was completed in silence. My confession had shocked the driver into mute submission. Everyone in the North Country was aware of the horrible accidents that had befallen my family and the conspiracy theories surrounding their deaths, but no one including the driver expected an heir to emerge so quickly, if at all.

Upon arrival in Bretton Woods, I asked the driver to pull into the scenic viewing area just opposite the entrance to my boyhood home. Stepping out of the car, I took in the panoramic view. The sweeping vista of Mount Washington towering above

10

the hotel at its foot was an exquisite sight to behold. Despite my reluctance to return, I had missed this view.

Tipping the driver, I decided to walk the remaining distance up to the red-roofed, bone-white landmark in order to prolong the feeling of solitude and to minimize any notion of grandeur that my arrival might elicit.

"It's an awfully long walk. You sure you don't want me to shuttle you up the entranceway?" the driver asked, hoping to be part of what I'm sure he anticipated to be a red-carpet arrival.

"No, I prefer to walk the grounds myself and casually arrive…unannounced."

Disappointed, the driver climbed back into the limo and exited onto Route 302. As the vehicle sped away in the distance, I crossed the byway, prepared to assault the mythical structure that had held people captive with intrigue for well over a hundred years. With each approaching step, the distance waned while an onslaught of memories lashed at me like a foreman's whip. The scars were still there, festering just below the surface. I only hoped the scabs I had built up after all these years could withstand the inevitable tempest that awaited me.

Despite my dawdling, I reached the hotel quicker than I expected. Bypassing the valet and the front entrance, I climbed the lesser-known side stairs hidden under the grand colonnaded veranda and emerged on the south porch. Looking out over the clay tennis courts and the bustling golf course clubhouse, I spied Crawford Notch looming in the distance. I had finally returned to the kingdom like an exiled noble seeking asylum amongst the protective woods of Bretton. I knew the answers I sought were hiding out here within the shadows of the hardwood forests. I just wasn't sure I wanted to find them.

"Trying to sneak in unannounced, are you?" a voice from behind me called.

Turning my head, I spied a sharply-dressed man. "You must be the world's oldest bellboy by now," I countered.

"Not anymore," he said with a laugh. "I tricked them into making me the head of security."

"No wonder this place has gone to hell in my absence."

"You're still full of spit and piss, aren't you? God, it's good to see you again, Darby."

"You too, Quinn."

"The hotel manager is itching to meet with you. She's been in quite a tizzy since learning you were planning on staying with us."

"I bet she is," I answered.

"It's not every day that a Medal of Honor winner graces us with their presence."

"Listen, do you think you could do me a favor, Quinn, and discreetly check me in? I'm exhausted and not in the mood for any pomp and circumstance the hotel manager might have planned."

"Already ahead of you, my friend," he said, holding up a key card, "but I better get a good tip because management is going to be pissed that I ruined their PR moment."

"Careful, they might fire you."

"I'm not that lucky," Quinn quipped, picking up my bag and shepherding me in through the ballroom entrance. After traversing the expansive room, we hung a left and climbed the back staircase up to the 3rd floor while chatting about old times and old friends. In the short amount of time it took to reach my room, I began to think that maybe my visit wouldn't be as bad as

I expected. This would be the first of many mistakes I would make.

CHAPTER 2

They say there's a high cost to always being right. Thankfully I lost my fear of being wrong a long time ago. Growing up, I was always known as a creative child. I found creative ways to get into trouble, and even more innovative ways to get out. My unique view of life followed me into adulthood. I'm still creative by God, but not as an artist; I'm celebrated as a killer. I think Hemingway had it half right. *You never kill anyone you want in a war.* You only kill yourself each and every day you survive. I wish I had died.

The so-called "lucky ones" survive in spite of themselves. I was taught that luck is when preparedness encounters opportunity. This mantra for living was drilled into my psyche throughout my younger years in Bretton Woods. I never questioned it and I most certainly never challenged it until that brutally oppressive summer. The scorched and blackened days of August flowed seamlessly into the equally harsh ill winds of a muted autumn, testing my adult faith in this ancient family truism.

La Niña had punished the North Country that summer, unleashing Mother Nature's version of the four horsemen of the apocalypse: heat, stifling humidity, sporadic rain, and the cursed black flies. The humidity tormented me as I lazily stretched out along the expansive veranda of the Mount Washington Hotel. Long shadows were forming along the ridgelines of the Presidential Range. The forecast was for thunderstorms tonight, big boomers with flashes of lightning. The kind of storm that sucks the breath right out of you. This evening's fury was supposed to finally usher in the cooler weather normally associated with New England's majestic fall foliage. I hoped the forecasters were right. We all needed the relief.

"Darby S. Weeks, that can't possibly be you," chortled a most bothersome voice, interrupting my fleeting moment of solitude.

"Hello, Silas," I replied disinterestedly, hoping he would move along and let me be.

"Well H-E double hockey sticks. The last time I saw you, I was asking for my five-iron. Are you still caddying? 'Cuz I could really use some help on that cursed 11th fairway."

"I haven't played golf in a long time," I admitted. "Listen, I was just enjoying the view and peacefulness of being alone so if you don't mind—"

"Looks like we're in for some rain," Silas interrupted as he sat down in the white wicker rocking chair next to me.

"That's what they're calling for," I replied with a frustrated sigh, realizing he was not going to leave me alone. I asked an innocent question that I regretted as soon as it left my mouth. "Are you still climbing the mountain every day, Silas?"

"A-yuh. Every day I go up and every day I come down. Right as rain. Haven't missed a day since '44. You know, you really should get back on the horse again. There's nothing to be afraid of from our little mountain. In fact, I'd wager that it might even improve your whole stink-eyed demeanor. If you don't mind me saying so, there's no sense in lollygagging around here all day like some god-forsaken leaf-peeping tourist, feeling sorry for yourself. Jeezum Crow, Darby! In my humble opinion, you need to…"

Oh god, please make him stop.

Silas Bollerud was junk mail personified: innocently packaged, but full of annoying crap that never stopped coming. He had to be at least a hundred and five in both years and pounds, but was still as sharp as a pricker bush. I couldn't believe he was still alive.

"Did you see the dinner menu for tonight? A travesty! A travesty indeed! That imbecile in cook's clothing is starting with a seared Quebec foie gras layered with an onion marmalade and crisp potatoes topped with a grape Muscat sauce, followed by a pan-roasted breast of pheasant, and braised legs with a duo of cabbage, fondant potato, and chanterelle Madeira sauce. Did you ever see such a lack of imagination? Why that same dish was just served in October of '44, to mixed reviews I might add."

"A travesty of the highest caliber," I half-heartedly replied, adding fuel to Silas' smoldering fire.

"That man should be shot for culinary plagiarism! That's the problem with society today. There is a lack of creativity and moral courage to do anything different. Speaking of moral courage, did I ever tell you what I did back in '44, Darby?"

16

Only a thousand times, I thought to myself, rolling my eyes.

"Just imagine what our Congress could accomplish if we got 'em all out of that miserable Washington and brought 'em here to the North Country. Once confronted with Yankee frugality and the awesome splendor of these Great North Woods, not to mention several of our friend Easton Crow's whiz bangs, Congress would surely find a way to end this asinine gridlock, pay down the skyrocketing national debt, and fix the blasted healthcare system. Did you know I was trying to check insurance rates on the government website the other day when I was redirected to FacePlace? Before I knew it, I was twerking with the supreme leader of the Democratic People's Republic of Korea."

"You were what?" I said, stifling a laugh.

"Twerking, I say…you know, a hundred and forty characters with hash browns."

"I think you mean tweeting, not twerking."

"Tweeting…twerking…it's all the same. Our country is a bloody mess. If I was President I would just make Easton the pharmaceutical czar and harvest his entire north forty. His magical drinks are the only healthcare we need around here. Are you listening to what I'm saying?"

Unfortunately, I had no choice but to listen. Where in the world was my drink?

"So what you're saying, Silas, is that you saved the world from financial ruin once and now you think you have the wherewithal to preserve the American way of life and health for me and my lethargic generation…yada, yada, yada."

"Don't be snide with me, Darby. If it wasn't for people like me, your snot-nosed generation would be pledging allegiance to Deutschland and doing the goose step instead of that crazy jitterbug."

Jitterbug? "Oh, the horror!" I quipped.

"You miserable ungrateful SOB," Silas snorted, shaking a fist at me. "If I was ten years younger I'd…"

I stopped listening as my drink mercifully arrived, the potent Witch Hazel Iced Gimlet. The WHIG consisted of frigid, pomegranate-flavored Stolichnaya vodka emulsified with just a pinch of Witch Hazel and topped off with a splash of lime. Easton's own magical concoction and one of my new vices in life. Antagonizing Silas was one of my old vices. Silas and I used to go through this ritualistic verbal sparring just about every day on the golf course. In my youth, I found him very entertaining, but tonight I had no patience or energy for his bantering. I was beat and all I wanted to do was sip at my medicinal drink, watch Mother Nature's impending lightshow, and turn in early. Luckily my flippant attitude caused Silas to lose his train of thought. Enraged and frustrated, the old man started stammering.

"Filth, flam, flam and filth!" he hissed. I contemptuously smiled, waiting for him to fire off his traditional parting salvo. "Balls…balls…and more balls!" Silas roared as he scurried away towards the bar. He would spend the rest of the evening chattering in poor Easton's ear, ranting and raving about what a smart-aleck bastard I was and how he would never speak to me again. I wondered why Easton didn't just slip some choke cherry leaves into one of old Silas' ginseng bourbons. In the blink of an eye, he could silence that windbag for good. The hundred dollar tips probably had something to do with Easton's saintly restraint. In any case, I knew Silas would be back tomorrow to engage me in another pointless conversation. I could count on it, right as rain to be sure.

Alone again, I sipped at my drink and stared out at the Presidential Range. The evening light had become a soft pink as the sun gracefully retreated westward, illuminating the dark underbelly of the menacing clouds forming above. The valley was in need of a good soaking rain and I was in need of a good night's sleep. Tonight's thunderstorm promised to deliver both.

Sleeping had become a distant stranger to me since my return. I'd spent the last few days here nursing old wounds. When I actually did sleep, night terrors hounded me. I wanted the memories in my head gone. Alleviation from the pain came from the most unlikely source: Easton Crow's potent elixirs. I'd been living off of my entirely unwelcomed fame and the goodwill of strangers who I once called friends. With each passing day I got a little closer to nothing, but at least I made it home.

The funeral was one meaningless conversation after another. People never know what to say in moments like that. It didn't matter, I wasn't listening anyway. We had calling hours in the Conservatory. My grandfather always called it "The Parlor." He loved that old room. He gave everything he had to this damn hotel. The governor came, so did a congressional delegation. It was the biggest social event Bretton Woods had ever seen. My grandfather was praised, he was honored, and then his ashes were hauled up the mountain, like an angel returning to heaven. Too bad I missed all of it. I only saw her.

"Time to batten down the hatches, Mr. Weeks. It's going to be a rough night," the bellboy lamented as he handed me a flashlight and continued on his way.

In more ways than one, I was starting to think.

The first flashes of lightning crackled their way across the darkened sky as the breeze began to freshen, chilling the

19

beads of sweat on my arms. The storm tonight would be violent as the seasons mingled and churned.

Faintly, I began to hear the orchestra play. Culinary plagiarism was now being served in the main dining room. I could only imagine the lather Silas had worked himself into by now. The music slowly became more discernible, and I started to recognize the haunting sounds of Vivaldi's *Four Seasons*. The angelic violins of the second concerto slowly crept down the expansive veranda, engulfing me like a warm wave in an ocean of memories, and then I thought of her. The music summoned her memory from the depths of my being, the way a familiar smell might conjure up remembrances of home.

"Emily," the name escaped my lips. Startled by my own mouth's betrayal, I repeated the infraction a second time as the music reached a crescendo, unleashing a torrent of emotion I could not control. Perhaps it was the enormity of all I had been through or the realization that I was alone for the first time in my life, but the tears came just as the rain began to fall. Colossal drops penetrated my soul while sheets of black water soaked the thirsty land all around me.

Damn you, Emily Baines.

CHAPTER 3

Quietly nestled behind the Mount Washington Hotel's grand staircase, the Rosebrook Bar is a sanctuary to the initiated. Its floor-to-ceiling windows offer unrivaled views of the Presidential range while its muted-colored walls and dark wood chairs are warmed by a cream and burgundy palette of color. It is a peaceful place of refuge from the never-ending ebb and flow of vacation-goers to the White Mountains.

"Darby?"

The voice was unmistakable. Soft and glowing, it lifted my heart while crushing my spirit. I last heard it a lifetime ago, in a state of love and trust, when my youthful arrogance embraced the unbridled passion in my heart. Its return was entirely unexpected. *The fates will find a way.*

"Darby?" the voice repeated.

Lowering my *Boston Globe*, I glanced up at perfection, but offered only scorn. I shook my head, thinking she could not possibly be here. Surely, the gods must jest.

"Darby, it's me...Emily."

I watched helplessly as the strands of time began to rewind before me. She had come to the funeral eighteen years earlier to pay her respects to my mother. She also came in hopes of mending old wounds, but only succeeded in heightening my own sense of loss. We never spoke that day, only making brief eye contact across the crowded parlor. In an instant, she knew the time wasn't right for us and I knew I loved her more than ever. She left as quickly as she had come, walking out of my life for a second time, trampling my heart with each retreating step she took, without ever uttering a word.

"Darby, please...say something...say anything," she pleaded.

"Prostibuli eligantia," I finally blurted out, *the elegance of a whore.*

The color drained from her face. She pursed her lips, prepared to lash out at me, then stopped herself. "Well, you always had a way with words," she replied, forcing a smile and sitting down at the table next to me. "Why are there so many pictures of animals in this room?" she asked, trying to make small talk with me after several minutes of awkward silence.

I looked up at the portrait of a white-footed mouse hanging on the wall above Emily's head. I smiled thinking how appropriate it was that the rat sitting next to me had the company of her own kind. Emily attempted several more conversation starters to no avail before she stood up, preparing leave.

22

"I know my presence here must be quite a shock, Darby, and I also realize you have many reasons to not want to talk to me, but I'm in town for a while and I would like to sort some things out with you if I can. You just need to give me a chance."

"You want a chance?" I said, feeling the anger boiling up inside of me. "What part of our history warrants you getting another chance?"

"It's been almost twenty years, and you still haven't let it go?" She shook her head. "That's really pathetic. You know what your biggest problem is? You only see things in black or white. Life is rarely that simple."

"Life is exactly that simple. You make choices and you have to live with those choices and everything that comes along with them."

"Sometimes good people suffer and bad people succeed. There are shades of gray in life that are more complex than you realize."

"Don't lecture me. I know more about life's complexities than you'll ever know, especially as it relates to life and death. So don't psychoanalyze me. Just leave, Emily. You're good at that."

She looked at me with hurt eyes. I had succeeded in denting her protective armor. Grabbing a bar napkin and a pen from her purse, Emily began to write. When she had finished, she handed me the makeshift note.

"As pleasant as this has been, I think we both need a little more time to process our emotions. Please think about meeting me on Wednesday. I wrote down the specifics about where I'll be and I hope you'll consider joining me."

As Emily exited the room, I crumbled the napkin in my fist and threw it on the floor without reading it. I would not give her another chance to break my heart.

Good riddance, Emily Baines.

***

Easton Crow was finishing up washing glasses on the other end of the Rosebrook Bar when he looked up and saw the alluring woman walk passed him and enter the room. She approached Darby and then hesitated, as if stuck in no man's land, trying to decide whether to flee or fight. Easton overheard her awkward one-sided conversation from across the room. His jaw hit the floor when Darby finally did speak. The woman took it surprisingly well. Easton liked her already.

Darby refused to talk, thwarting the woman's attempts to start a conversation. Finally stymied, she grabbed a bar napkin and scribbled out a note. She handled it to Darby and told him that she would be waiting. He dropped it on the floor without even reading it after the woman had walked away. Fortunately, Easton was wise enough to pick it up.

***

Jefferson, NH – Planning Board Meeting

"Seeing the existence of a quorum, and a packed house I might add," the chairman of the planning board said while adjusting his glasses and gazing out at the throng of residents eager to speak at tonight's meeting, "we shall move on to old business."

"Mr. Chairman, at the last meeting we tabled the discussion of Aqua-Nord's proposal to build power transmission lines through part of Cherry Pond and its associated wetlands. I move that we reopen the discussion and get further input from all interested parties," droned the planning board secretary.

"Very well, I will second that. Mr. Robarge, do you have an opening statement you would like to share with the planning board?"

"Yes. Thank you, Mr. Chairman," Jacques Robarge said with confidence, ignoring a scattering of boos and cat calls. "Aqua-Nord's Granite Pass project will have many positive benefits for the community of Jefferson and the surrounding areas that I would like to state for the record."

"Please continue," the chairman said.

"The Granite Pass project will improve air quality for healthy trees and more importantly, for the children who play under them. We all contribute to the culture, society, and economy that makes these Great North Woods a special place and we all care when changes are proposed to this place we call home, but sometimes changes need to occur in order to solve the tough challenges facing our communities and our families. In these uncertain economic times, The Granite Pass project will create more than twelve hundred jobs for New Hampshire residents. Surveyors, line workers, construction workers and the industry that supports them all will have cold, hard cash in their pockets. The project will generate twenty-five million dollars in additional tax revenues for schools, public safety, and to help maintain the infrastructure of New Hampshire. That means improving our libraries, keeping the snowplows moving, and fixing our roads after long winters. The Granite Pass project will provide us with twelve hundred megawatts of clean, reliable energy. That's enough to reduce carbon dioxide emissions by up to five million tons a year - equal to the annual emissions of nine hundred thousand cars. More importantly, this is the affordable and sustainable energy you need to attract new businesses to your town and support new manufacturing throughout the region. At

25

the end of the day, this discussion is not just about energy; it's about jobs and local tax revenues. It's about a sustainable future for the place we all call home – The Great North Woods."

A silence followed, broken by a slow, unenthusiastic clap as a man in the back of the room stood up preparing to speak. "Mr. Chairman, may I respond?"

"State your name and move to the microphone, please," the chairman directed.

"My name is Finnegan Shamus Doyle and I would like to ask Mr. Robarge a few clarifying questions."

"Mr. Chairman, I object," snorted Robarge. "This man is a known eco-terrorist who will stop at nothing to protect a bog full of blood-sucking mosquitoes. Hell, I don't even think he's a resident of your community. He should not be allowed to speak."

"Mr. Doyle, can you please state your place of residence for the record?" the chairman asked.

"I was born and raised in New Hampshire and I am a resident of the Pliny Range and the Kilkenny's. I also am a resident of Cherry Mountain, the Dartmouth Range, and the Presidentials looming boldly in the distance. I inhabit the tranquil Israel River valley and the many mountain streams that flow into it. Oh, and by the way, I also have a PO Box in town," Finnegan said, glaring at Robarge.

"He sounds like a resident to me," the chairman admitted. "Please continue, Mr. Doyle."

Robarge rolled his eyes and popped an antacid tablet into his mouth.

"I would like to ask Mr. Robarge how long he has been a resident of New Hampshire."

"I am not a resident of New Hampshire," Robarge answered.

"Oh, well then can you tell me how many years have you been visiting our great state?"

"This is my first time in New Hampshire," confessed Robarge.

"Oh, so where is it that you call home?"

"I'm French," Robarge said with pride. "I was born in Marseille, but currently live in the Lac-Saint-Charles area just north of Quebec."

"I'm confused. Didn't you just say in your opening statement some babble about 'a place we all call home – the Great North Woods'? Were you lying then or are you lying now?" Finnegan pressed.

"Mr. Chairman, I came here to talked about the benefits of the Granite Pass project, not to discuss my—"

"No, you came here to spew out a bunch of hooey trying to convince everyone you're a flannel wearing, moose hunting, maple syrup tapping local good ole boy who has a shared interest and concern with our scenic vistas and unassuming charm. You're nothing more than a carpet bagger and snake oil salesman!" Finnegan shouted, working the crowd into a frenzy mob.

"Booo!!!" the crowd roared in unison.

"Go home, Frog!" a voice rang out as anger began to circulate through the room.

Finnegan sat down and smiled. He had accomplished his goal and his work was done for the night.

Zut alors! Jacques Robarge thought to himself while massaging his temples. *My employer is not going to be happy.*

CHAPTER 4

To call Pickford Marsh a robber baron would be grossly understating his power, not to mention it would be incredibly offensive to robber barons the world over. Unlike his predecessors, the medieval noblemen whose majestic castles overlooked the Rhine, Pickford's wealth was impalpable and nearly invisible. He despised public grandeur, preferring to work and live in the shadows of society. His business practices were ruthless. He was the ultimate puppet master, pulling strings to get what he wanted. Rivals equally hated and admired Pickford's tenacity. Few ever said 'no' to Pickford Marsh or his international conglomerate, Aqua-Nord.

"Robarge!" Pickford screamed into the phone. "What's holding up my permits?"

"Mr. Marsh, I apologize for the delay, but the town planning boards of Jefferson and Gorham have tabled your permit requests until their environmental impact studies have been completed. I expect—"

"I expect you to do the goddamn job I'm paying you to do," Pickford cursed into the phone. "Grease the wheels and make it happen. I've had enough of these delays. We're already behind schedule. Get it done or you're done!"

"It will be done, but—" The drone of the dial tone announced the end of their discussion. Jacques Robarge put down the phone and poured himself a double scotch. This dog and pony show was giving him an ulcer. He wished he had never heard of Pickford Marsh or Aqua-Nord.

***

Imbeciles. I'm surrounded by imbeciles, thought Pickford as he paced around his office. Robarge had become ineffective and a liability as a result. Pickford wasn't going to let some two-bit committee delay his work. Didn't they know what this would mean for them and their communities? It's money, jobs, and progress. It was time to reeducate the denizens of these northern dirt farms.

"Martha!" he yelled into the intercom. "Get me Giselle on the line, pronto!" Giselle could fix this. It would cost him, but it would be well worth it. It was time to take out the trash.

***

My heart rate spiked and dipped as I paced around the Marshfield Base Station. Even though my mind was already made up, that inner voice in my head kept telling me to steer clear of the past. The voice had saved me numerous times in the killing fields of conflict, strife, and destruction. My own guardian angel shielding me from harm's way, telling me to go left when others went right. Sometimes I listened, but most of the time I just dove headlong into one big hot mess after another.

Reaching into my pocket, I removed the bar napkin that Easton had retrieved for me from the Rosebrook Bar's floor. I reread Emily's handwritten note as a fire reignited inside of me. The penmanship was immaculate and it smelled like a fresh breeze off the warm summer ocean. Waves of regret continued to twinge inside me. What in the world was I doing here?

The noise of an imperial blue cog railcar exiting the station jarred me from the thought. It was crammed full of leaf-peeping tourists ascending to the summit of Mount Washington. The conductor launched into his canned monologue about how the mountain was home to the world's worst weather and that their car would be the last one making the journey up the three mile long trestle this afternoon. Large thunderclouds were popping all over Vermont to the west and it was only a matter of time before they assaulted the North Country.

I shouldered my worn backpack and shuffled towards the trail sign, hoping I would encounter something, anything that would change my mind. The US Forest Service sign offered no such help. I read it with a sigh.

Ammonoosuc Rivine Trail. Lakes of the Clouds Hut – 2.4 miles

The AMC hut on the edge of the Lakes of the Clouds was one of the more challenging resting spots to reach in all of the Great North Woods. I'd hiked this scenic trail many times in my youth, and loved the views of cascading waterfalls that it afforded. The hut itself was located above the tree line on the southern shoulder of Mount Washington. Intrepid hikers who reached the hut were rewarded with sweeping views of the valley below. The sensory experience was enhanced by magnificent sunsets that I imagined would have inspired the paintings of J. M. W. Turner. At night, the eerie and mesmerizing Northern Lights would serpentine overhead, making even the most devout atheist question their beliefs. Mother Nature's greatness had a way of humbling travelers to the North Country.

The Lakes of the Clouds was also a place where young lovers would frolic in the high altitude pools, admiring a different type of beauty. The last time I made the journey here, I was a brash, hard-bodied nineteen-year-old. I remember that Emily and I made the strenuous climb in record time. We couldn't keep our hands off each other. Our bodies were bronzed with deep tan lines from a long, scorching summer. Two carefree lovers dripping wet after a day of swimming in the two tarns that made up the Lakes of the Clouds. As the sun's final rays flickered and retreated behind the westward mountains of Vermont in the distance, purple and orange pastel clouds strolled above us as we stretched out on the rocks at the water's edge. We would lie awake all night under the panoramic stars, exploring each other's body, feeling like the only two people left on Earth. We were immortal beings making promises to each other that I knew we wouldn't keep come the dawn. It was like a Technicolor dream from long ago. I was never quite sure if it was even real. So my reappearance back here some twenty years later, as a middle-aged man without a profession, was quite unsettling.

Since arriving home, I'd come to realize that I'd been homesick every day for a place I wasn't even sure existed anymore. Now, presented with the opportunity to finally return, I felt nonplussed. What if the reality paled in comparison to the memory? *Time to find out*, I told myself as I set out climbing into an inverted abyss.

31

The climb was even more challenging than I remembered, but I reached my destination with an hour of daylight to spare. *Not bad, Weeks, not bad at all*, I congratulated myself as I pushed open the door to the gray lodging hut and entered the building. I was expecting a throng of people inside since the hut could house over ninety guests in twin bunkhouses. It should have been full of flannel and backpacks during this time of year. The silence of the place was unnerving. There was not a soul stirring. The wooden benches and long tables stood empty. Outside, the rumble of thunder signaled an abrupt change to the weather. Not uncommon on Mount Washington. To be caught above the tree line when the weather turned fierce was almost surely a death sentence to the unprepared.

I walked with caution over to one of the side windows of the dining room and was without warning blinded by a flash of lightning that struck the trailhead above the hut. The accompanied *boom* of the thunderclap that followed knocked me off my feet. It shook the floor and rattled the stacked dinner dishes of the hut, causing an immense sense of dread in me. Regaining my vision and my composure, I rose to my feet and started to explore the rustic dining room. A large framed sign on the opposite wall caught my eye. Moving closer, I noticed a smaller plaque off to one side that looked weathered and tarnished. My curiosity piqued, I headed towards it as another streak of lightning and crack of thunder pounded the hut causing me to stumble into the far wall. Close enough now to read the weathered plaque, I realized it was a poem.

STORM FEAR
When the wind works against us in the dark,
And pelts with snow

32

The lowest chamber window on the east,
And whispers with a sort of stifled bark,
The beast,
Come out! Come out!'-
It costs no inward struggle not to go,
Ah, no!
I count our strength,
Two and a child,
Those of us not asleep subdued to mark
How the cold creeps as the fire dies at length,-
How drifts are piled,
Dooryard and road ungraded,
Till even the comforting barn grows far away
And my heart owns a doubt
Whether 'tis in us to arise with day
And save ourselves unaided.

- Robert Frost

"How appropriate," I said aloud to myself.

"I never did like Frost," a female voice echoed from across the room.

Startled, I turned towards the sound behind me. Emily was perched alone on top of one of the large wooden picnic tables. Her seductive blue eyes penetrated me, inviting me to step back into an ancient memory. I stared at her for a long moment trying to think of something significant to say, but my mind was blank.

"Did you know Frost was originally from California?" I finally managed to get out as another volley of thunder detonated, rattling the windows and causing me to duck for cover.

Emily laughed at my awkwardness. She had the type of laugh that was contagious and intoxicating all at once. I felt like I was nineteen again. She reached into her backpack achingly slow without removing her eyes from me and pulled out an enticing bottle of Pappy Van Winkle, its age matching the number of years I'd been away.

"I thought this might make getting reacquainted easier," she said, undoing the top button of her blouse.

I shook my head. "That will only guarantee I don't remember anything tomorrow."

"Maybe that's best with what I'm planning on doing to you," she said with a mischievous twinkle in her eye.

God help me, I thought to myself. I'm so going to regret this hot mess.

***

"The heir is already in the North Country," the voice hissed through the speakerphone in Pickford Marsh's office. "His presence is an imminent threat to both you and me. He must not be allowed to stay. Force him to leave or make the necessary arrangements and see to it that he joins the others in the Pit of Hell and the Well of Lost Souls."

"Listen, I have other headaches right now that are bigger priorities," Pickford began. "The Stickney boy is no threat to me. There's nothing left for him here in the North Country. I'm not worried at all. He knows nothing. The coward will run away like he did as a child. He's unable to face his fears."

"Do not be so confident Iscariot. The Stickney family remains strong and continues to have many supporters who would like nothing better than to see you destroyed."

"Ha! I'm worth billions. I'm all-powerful and untouchable. Nobody can destroy me," Pickford said with arrogance.

"I can destroy you and your family fortune in the blink of an eye!" roared the voice. "You will listen and obey me if you value your life."

Pickford swallowed hard, squashing his self-adulation. It annoyed him to no end that he had to be subservient to the voice on the other end of the line. He'd play along for a while, at least until he got the opportunity to bury this thorn in his side. "What do want me to do?"

"The priest knows much. He is an ally of the family and he now possesses the riddles. He must be prevented from giving them to the heir and placing him on the path of discovery. Find and destroy the riddles," the voice commanded.

"As you wish," Pickford replied as the line went dead.

***

The storm continued to bellow in the dark outside the bunkhouse as Emily ran her fingers down my taut back, examining each new bump and scar with fascination. She poked at several healed exit wounds and multiple scars. Her hands hovered over the remnants of a once-deep slash. One of her fingers slowly traced the outline of rough skin that traveled down my shoulder blade to the top of my hip.

"Does this still hurt?" she asked in hushed tones while slowly kissing the raised ridge.

"No," I replied half asleep, "the pain is long gone. Now it's just a souvenir from another life."

"I think scars are sexy. So manly," she purred as she kissed my back again.

I laughed into the pillow, thinking about all the scars I had that she couldn't see. "I don't feel manly today…just broken and old."

Emily looked at me for a moment with quizzical eyes. "You know the Japanese have a wonderful word called *wabi-sabi*."

"*Wabi-sabi*," I repeated, my eyelids growing heavy as my body yearned for sleep.

"Essentially it means finding beauty in imperfection," she said, fingering my scars again. "When something breaks or shatters, like a cup or a dish, the Japanese mend the broken pieces together and fill in the cracks with gold. They aggrandize the damage because they believe broken objects are more beautiful than new ones. Broken things have an appealing story to them."

"Fascinating," I mumbled, losing my battle with sleep.

"Just like the broken parts of us, Darby," she whispered, resting her head on my chest. "The scars and imperfections make us who we are. They make us more interesting and beautiful. I think that's why I'm so drawn to you, scars and all. I know you won't believe me, but I still love you even after all these years. That's why this is so incredibly hard for me."

I didn't hear Emily's last words clearly. Months of irregular sleep patterns due to debilitating stress and a half bottle of bourbon had finally caught up with me. I faded into never-never land, dreaming I was a broken shot glass in a cupboard full of fine china, my cracks hastily spackled with fools' gold. No matter how hard Emily tried, I would always be a lonesome weed amongst the flowers of the North Country.

CHAPTER 5

The light was pain-inducing and mesmerizing all at once as it
woke me from an uneasy slumber. Stumbling out of my bunk,
the early rays of morning greeted me like senators with daggers. I
shook the thought from my head while I drew open the ripped
shade of a bunkhouse window. A thick layer of fog had encased
the valley below, reinforcing the fact that I was elevated more
than 5000 feet above the civilization sleeping below. It was like
looking down from a gargoyle's perch. Weather observers on top
of Mount Washington called the socked-in cloud cover below an
undercast. How appropriate, I thought, since I felt insufficiently
skilled and not at all anxious to descend into my former life.
Bretton Woods harbored too many ghosts. They didn't need
another walking amongst them.

Looking down I noticed an envelope stuffed into my empty boot. I shook my head; another goodbye letter from Emily to add to my growing collection. I sat down on my bunk and ripped open the note.

Darby –

Thank you for a memorable night…and morning, you stud! I had to run, important conference call this morning. Let's rendezvous for dinner and drinks tonight in the Main Dining Room. There are some important things I need to tell you. Wear a nice suit or you know who will never let you in.

Hugs & Kisses – Em

I closed my bloodshot eyes and nearly hurled at the thought of another drink. A splitting headache coupled with that annoying voice in my head screaming *I told you so*, made me think twice about attending this get together. She knows I don't have a suit. *He couldn't refuse entry to a veteran?*

I reluctantly got dressed, repacked my bag and headed out to the hut's rustic dining room, hoping to scrounge up something to eat from the rudimentary kitchen.

"Coffee?"

Thinking I was alone, the simplicity of the question caught me off guard. My cliché answer did not. "High octane if you got it."

"You're as constant as the North Star." Elsie Fitzgerald smirked before handing me a cup of java goodness.

"And you, my dear, have saved my ass," I murmured, grateful for the caffeine.

Elsie Fitzgerald was the known to all in the North Country as the Mountain Matriarch. From Lonesome Lake to

Carter Notch, she oversaw the care of all eight of the AMC White Mountain huts. East German by birth, Elsie's parents fled the oppression of the Iron Curtain when she was nine years old. They immigrated to the United States and eventually settled in the White Mountains of New Hampshire since it reminded them of their native Ore Mountains in Bohemia. Elsie was as strong as a teak tree with stunning beauty for her age. As an avid Red Sox fan, she would frequently put condescending and haughty male New Yorkers to shame by challenging them to arm wrestling contests. After stomping them physically, she would crush their spirit by making them wear Fenway apparel for the duration of their visit. Those humbled by Elsie affectionately called her by another moniker – The Green Monster.

"You look like pure hell, Darby."

"Well, I'm not twenty anymore."

"Are you sure?" she said, picking up the empty bottle of Pappy Van Winkle and a pair of black lace panties.

"Oh, sorry about the mess."

"Had fun last night, did we?" Elsie said with a grin, and her green eyes sparkled.

"To tell you the truth, I don't remember much," I said, massaging my head.

"Ah, well you've earned some fun from what I've heard. We're all proud to have a hero back home safe and sound."

I nodded in silent agreement before deciding to change the subject.

"I'm going to go see Flavio tonight at the hotel."

"Be careful with that one," she warned. "He gets his feelings hurt when a celebrity is in town and they don't immediately grace his precious dining room."

"Well, what do you expect? He's a self-made man with a lot of pride."

"Self-made man, hah!" Elsie bellowed.

I took the bait and asked, "What's wrong with a self-made man?"

"They only worship their creator," Elsie hissed.

I winced at the obvious jab. She knew without doubt that I thought of myself as being self-made. I never took anything from anyone, preferring to live life on my own terms. I stared down at Elsie, trying to decide if I should flee or fight. I decided to play it safe and quit while I was behind. I sipped at my steaming coffee and thought about how many times I had walked these same planks of wood with my father and grandfather.

"You know," Elsie said, sensing my loneliness, "we all miss loved ones who have passed, but you have to keep the faith. You'll see them again soon."

That's what I fear.

"Do you ever get tired of trying to keep all of these old huts up and running?" I asked, changing the subject once again.

"Never," she said with an infectious smile. "I get to walk every day in God's country – no walls, no phone, and no schedule. I come and go as I please."

"It sounds lonely to me. You have no complaints at all?" I asked in disbelief, trying to picture myself in her shoes.

"It depends on your perspective, my dear sweet boy." She touched my hand and coldness shot up my arm.

"How so?" I asked, looking for wisdom in the crows' feet of her deep-set eyes.

She exhaled slowly and then continued. "There used to be

a framed picture of President Abraham Lincoln that hung in my parents' house not too far from here. On the picture was written, 'We can complain because rose bushes have thorns, or rejoice because rose bushes have thorns.' I only see roses in life, Darby. From a distance, the thorns cease to exist. This is how I choose to live."

I nodded. "It's a shame they didn't name one of these peaks after Lincoln. He deserves to be honored here."

"Even if it would have made him feel uncomfortable to accept such an honor?" Elsie asked while opening a drawer in the kitchen and removing an envelope.

"Yes, it's not his choice," I said with conviction.

"I'm happy to hear you say that, Senior Chief," she said beaming as she laid down a newspaper clipping containing a photograph of me receiving the Medal of Honor. "Allow people to honor you, Darby. You must realize it's for their benefit and not yours." Then she kissed me gently on the cheek before turning and walking towards the door. "Now get the hell out of my hut and go take a hot shower. You smell like a whore's handbag—" she mockingly yelled at me, "—and take these wretched panties with you!"

CHAPTER 6

Dinner is a celebrated event at the Mount Washington Hotel. Entering the main dining room is like traveling back in time. Guests are required to dress for dinner and a full orchestra accompanies each course.

The dining room as a whole reminds me of a gigantic Tiffany lamp. At sunset, brilliant pastel hues penetrate the stained glass infused room, cascading light in every direction. Tonight was no different. A kaleidoscope of color courtesy of Mother Nature and the flamboyant Flavio Chiapetti blinded me. Flavio's dinner jackets were almost as famous as the hotel itself. Tonight he was outfitted in a lavender sharkskin coat accessorized with a lime green handkerchief. He greeted each guest like a long lost relative flashing a pearly white smile that reminded me of a great white shark sizing up its next meal. Flavio had ruled this dining room for over four decades. All powerful, he alone decided who gained entrance, where they sat, and how long they had to wait for their food. He knew everyone and by God everyone knew him. He was a matchmaker who led people to their destinies, whether they were prepared for it or not.

Arriving early, I stood outside the confluence of three rooms gazing down one hallway and looking up at the balcony. The Princess stared back down at me, offering no advice. The portrait had always unnerved me. Was she judging me too? I found the expectations of my childhood home suffocating and evaded the preordination by enlisting in the Navy. Little did I know, my destiny had already been determined. The medal only sealed my fate.

I moved to the right and continued down the hallway, scanning the dining room for someone congenial to share a table with me until Emily made her entrance. I saw no one of interest, but I heard Silas a mile away.

"Maine salmon filet with a wasabi, shiitake glaze on woodland mushrooms with sautéed bok choy, shrimp croquettes and yuzu citrus sauce!" he bellowed in disbelief while theatrically performing hari-kari with his butter knife.

"Silas is in rare form tonight. The chef is going to kill that old kook one of these days," I uttered to no one in particular.

"From your mouth to God's ear," Flavio replied as he returned from the kitchen. "To what do I owe the honor of your presence tonight, Senior Chief?" he said, looking me up and down and eyeing my dress blue uniform.

"Hello, my old friend," I said with a smile. "A thousand apologies for taking so long to visit you." I extended my hand, hoping my uniform would meet Flavio's rigorous standards of decorum.

43

"Do you have a reservation?" he responded, not looking up from his scheduling book.

This is not going well, I thought to myself. "I'm meeting someone later and I was hoping I could wait in your magnificent room and admire the views. Anyone flying solo tonight?" I was hoping Flavio would take pity on me.

"Hmm, let's see. I have a butter knife wielding Samurai, an egotistical amnesiac, or a foul-mouthed man of the cloth. Pick your poison," he said smugly, looking me directly in the eye. I glanced over my shoulder at Silas. The ritualistic suicide had finally ended. He had moved on to accosting the dessert tray. I exhaled and then accepted my penance.

"A little religion and food never hurt anyone," I mused.

"Tell it to Jesus." Flavio smirked as he led me to my destiny.

The room parted like the ocean before the bow of a mighty warship as he led me to the far end of the dining room. I was hoping to make it to my seat without drawing any undue attention to myself. Unfortunately Flavio had other plans. With a snap of his fingers, the orchestra broke into *Anchors Aweigh* and every eye in the dining room was staring at that little medal hanging from my neck. A thunderous applause broke out as the room rose to their feet. Strangers shook my hand and slapped me on the back as I passed. I caught the waitress' eye and sent out a distress signal. Liquid courage was on the way. Finally reaching my table by the window, I exhaled again feeling queasy. *Well, it can't get any worse.*

"Why the hell weren't you at church this morning?" thundered Father Thaddeus Callaghan as he puffed away on a Macanudo.

"Um...well, maybe because I'm not religious," I said defensively while taking my seat.

"Likely excuse," he grumbled. "I need butts in the seats and with that entrance you just made, you could clearly draw a crowd for me. Hell, for a minute I thought Admiral Nimitz himself had walked through the door."

"Shouldn't Jesus' words draw a crowd for you?" I asked innocently.

"Don't tell me my business, boy! Attendance has been down since these cowardly acts of terrorism started. I'm beginning to think people are afraid to congregate in large groups."

With caution I began to say, "Well...maybe if you didn't lock the doors right after church started you'd get a larger—"

"Moose shit!" he hollered just a little too loud for my comfort level.

"Took the words right out of my mouth!" Silas fired back from across the room as he spit out one of the chef's chocolate creations.

"Heretics, all of them. What could be more important than celebrating the Gospel and giving thanks to the Lord? Jesus doesn't wait for no one and neither does my tee time, Darby," he said, blowing smoke rings in my face.

I peered across the room at Flavio and caught a glimpse of him grinning from ear to ear. He was enjoying this a little too much. The waitress mercifully arrived with our drinks. Father Callaghan was double-fisting tonight: Ginko Pinkos and Balsam Bourbons. Easton Crow's Ginkgo Pinko was a Cuba Libre energized with a pinch of Ginkgo biloba. He marketed it as a true memory enhancer, but Father Callaghan drank them to ease the symptoms of tinnitus he had suffered with since his days as a

45

Navy chaplain in Vietnam. There is nothing worse than an alert drunk who can read lips.

Turning serious for a moment, Callaghan leaned in and whispered in his pebble-filled voice, "I'm worried, Darby. I haven't seen senseless violence like this since 'Nam. Something is brewing. I can feel it in my bones just like I could sense when the VC were sneaking in through the wire at our firebase. I fear my life is in danger. Do you know someone broke into the Rectory last night and ransacked the place?"

"Why would anybody want to break into a church or hurt you?" I asked.

"They were looking for something," Callaghan replied while pulling an object out of his jacket pocket and placing it on the table in front of me.

"A grasshopper?" I observed.

Callaghan let out a raucous cackle that cascaded into a long hacking cough. He stymied the irritation by swallowing the remains of his brilliant amber libation. His eyes refocused on me. "Bourbon is not for the timid drinker," he announced before inverting his Glencairn glass and encasing the insect between us.

"The meek prefer Vodka," I retorted, knocking back my own liquid fortification. I stared at him, watching beads of sweat escape from his forehead. I'd seen enough scared men to realize he wasn't sick, but shaken with fear.

"Cicada," he said, pointing to the glass. "The seventeen-year locust. The infant of the species burrows into the ground until it finds new roots from which to feed on. It wallows in the dirt for 17 years. Then the nymph emerges from hiding and molts, shedding its hardened shell. Only after freeing itself of its old skin can it finally become an adult."

"Fascinating," I lied.

46

Callaghan set his jaw, picked up his glass and slammed it back down on the table, decapitating the bug. "Don't patronize me, boy!" he shouted.

The room went silent as all eyes focused on the commotion at our table. Turning my head, I announced to the room, "Never bet against Notre Dame in the presence of a priest." The crowd laughed as the orchestra broke into the Golden Domer's Victory March.

"Everything all right, Senior Chief?" Flavio asked with raised eyebrows.

"We're fine," I replied as I returned my gaze to Callaghan. "Okay, Father. You have my attention."

"Do you know what the cicada does as soon as it becomes an adult?"

I sighed. "Eat?"

"No, it mates and then it quickly dies."

"What are you trying to tell me?" I asked, growing tired of his science lecture.

"Do you ever wonder about your father, Darby?"

"Every second of every day," I answered with hurt eyes.

"Your father and grandfather did things to protect you, Darby. Things you couldn't possibly understand as a child. They entrusted me with a certain knowledge and made me promise that when the time was right I would set you on the correct path to enlightenment."

"What does that mean?" I asked with an aching heart.

"Rebirth."

"I don't understand."

"Study the cicada. It will put you on the path to discovery."

47

Father Callaghan's cryptic message frustrated me to no end. If he had knowledge about my family, why couldn't he just tell me what it was? Why all the secrecy?

"Did you tell the authorities about the break-in or your concerns about your safety?" I asked, sipping at my drink.

"Yes, they came and did a cursory walk around, but the sheriff said it was probably just a bunch of drunk kids bored on a Friday night."

"Did he identify any suspects?" I was wondering why anyone would consider it fun to ransack a church.

"Oh, just the usual riff raff. That Doyle boy is a person of interest according to the sheriff."

"Finn? You mean Finnegan Doyle? Is he still around?" I asked, experiencing a sensation I hadn't felt since my time in the tribal lands of Afghanistan.

"Yes, that boy returned about a year or so ago. The bastard was in jail out in Oregon somewhere waiting to be arraigned for environmental sabotage."

"What in the world is environmental sabotage?"

"Spiking trees, arson, destroying construction equipment…etcetera," he said, fluttering his hand above his head.

"Like environmental terrorism?"

"Yes, exactly. As I recall, he was mixed up with a group called the Earth Liberation Front. They referred to themselves as ELF but they had nothing to do with peace on Earth and goodwill to all men. That thug should be locked up for life in a federal prison with his tree-hugger friends."

"Why isn't he?" I asked.

"Rumor has it some mysterious benefactor paid for a legal dream team and the charges were dropped because of some rat ass technicality," Callaghan said with a belch.

I remembered reading about ELF and their tactics. According to the FBI, the group was the nation's leading domestic terror threat, even more dangerous than Al Qaeda. They had been accused of committing over twelve hundred acts of eco-terrorism over the last decade alone. How did Finn get mixed up with the likes of them? "So he just moved back here?" I asked.

"He had nowhere else to go, I guess. He was living at his step daddy's place, but as you can image that didn't go over too well."

"Is he still there?"

"No, he got kicked out. Last I heard he went off the grid, living in the wilderness somewhere out there in the dark."

"And you think he's responsible for not only the church break-in, but all the trouble Aqua-Nord is having around here?" I asked, putting the pieces together.

"I don't think, I *know!*" Callaghan barked, then he knocked back the last of his drink while slipping off his chair.

I helped Father Callaghan to his feet. "I'm calling it a night, Padre. Why don't you go get you some sleep? You'll feel better in the morning."

"If I live that long," he sputtered. He looked directly through me, into a place only known to those who have endured the horrors of combat. "If I die, seek out the knowledge, follow the riddles."

I shook my head. "You're talking nonsense, Father. Let's get you home."

"I don't need any help. I can find my own way home." Callaghan gingerly took a few steps and staggered toward the door. He stopped momentarily and turned back toward me. "Study the cicada. I'd hate to see you lose your head too," he said ominously before continuing out the door.

I sat there for a minute pondering everything Callaghan had said to me as Flavio approached the table. Slapping me on the back, he handed me a note. I didn't have to read it to know what it said. Emily wasn't coming. She stood me up again.

***

A clear moonless night settled over the valley as the temperature began to plummet. Darkness came early this time of year in the North Country and the saboteur knew there was no time to waste. The figure clad in black maneuvered silently in and out of the clearing, weaving between the heavy machinery and trucks as weighty puffs of breath hung in the air.

The plan was simple enough. Very fine particles of aluminum oxide would be poured into the fuel lines of the trucks. The soft metal grit would circulate throughout the vehicle's engine, chewing out pieces of the cylinders and pistons. The trucks would be inoperable shortly after they started up. The bulldozers and excavators required more complicated methods to assure their utter destruction. With methodical precision, the saboteur drained diesel fuel from each machine, soaking rolls of cotton rags with the brackish liquid. The soaked rags were then placed in and round the machine's engine, under exposed wiring, along the hoses, next to the gauges, in the treads, wheels, and in the cab itself. Finally the behemoth was showered in the remaining fuel and ignited using a gasoline filled Molotov cocktail. It would burn like a Nordic funeral pyre until all that was left was melted metal and a charred shell.

A proper sacrifice to Mother Earth, thought the arsonist. The flames began to grow higher as the heat penetrated the blackness of the night. *Pickford Marsh's days are numbered. He will be made to suffer like the throngs who felt the heavy boot of his oppression and sins.* Justice was at hand.

***

Solitude and loneliness are two completely different things. The word 'loneliness' conjures up visions of suffering and pain, but 'solitude' to me is really an expression of joy. It's joyful to be alone because it means you have fewer problems and I decided that Emily was one problem I could do without.

After finishing my dinner in blissful solitude, I sat facing the orchestra, relishing the opportunity to watch complete strangers waltz while the musicians played on. I thought about the pace of life and how not more than a hundred years ago the scene unfolding before me in this dining room was commonplace for the rich. Life was a lot less complicated with fewer distractions in the grand age of coal and steel. Electricity and the innovation that it spurred really screwed things up for humanity.

I swirled ice cubes in my Waterford crystal glass and thought about the significance of where I was seated tonight. Thomas Edison sat in this very same dining room on the night the hotel originally opened. He was the first to toast Joseph Stickney and his vision to create this grand hotel, a northern playground for the rich. Edison never led men in battle, but he exerted more power than any conqueror the world had ever known. His emblem was a dove of peace, but his inventions, in

51

my opinion, killed what it truly meant to be human. He was a slayer of solitude.

Standing up, I began to meander towards the door, hoping to escape unnoticed. Unfortunately my departure was just as drawn out as my entrance had been as patrons lined up to shake my hand once again and thank me for my service. Luckily, the numerous libations I had ingested made my exit a lot less painful, but I still couldn't wait to remove my uniform and that damn medal that hung around my neck like an albatross. As I cleared the dining room and neared the lobby, another voice ensnared me, preventing my escape.

"Mr. Weeks, a word please," said the hotel manager. Ushering me into the Princess Lounge, Georgina Sinclair directed me to a seat at the bar. The room was empty as the dining room's late seating was well underway. Easton Crow was busy washing glasses behind the bar. Georgina poured herself a coffee and asked me what I wanted to drink. Feeling nostalgic at the sight of all the green bottles hanging on the wall, I ordered an absinthe. Easton looked at his boss, seeking her approval.

"Get the good stuff," she commanded as she turned and closed the door leading into the dining room. Easton sprinted from his position behind the bar and returned a few moments later with a shimmering flagon containing the emerald-colored liquid. The bottle of Absinthe Verte de Fougerolles ensured that I'd have no problem sleeping tonight. Hell, if I was really lucky, I might not wake up at all.

Easton prepared two substantial glasses of the green goodness with precision. Pouring in the electric liquid, the smell of anise and thujone filled the air. Satisfied that the proportions were correct, he balanced a delicate cube of pure sugar cane on top of a slotted spoon and slowly began to dissolve it with a bottle of Hildon natural mineral water. The British water was prized for its purity and achieved its well-balanced taste by taking more than fifty years to percolate through the chalk hills of the Hampshire countryside. When both glasses had been concocted, Easton placed one in front of me, but left the second glass where it stood on the bar. Georgina dismissed Easton, telling him she would finish cleaning up and sent him home for the evening.

"So what did you want to talk about?" I asked after taking a sip of the wormwood-infused liquid.

"You've been ignoring me."

"I've been ignoring everyone," I sighed, "don't take it personally."

Glancing at the open doorway adjacent to the hallway, Georgina reached for the second glass and took a healthy sip.

"Ms. Sinclair, I'm shocked," I said, feigning disapproval.

"If you had to run this hotel you'd drink too," she said with weary eyes. "There are some matters that need to be discussed."

I nodded my head, understanding the conversation that was about to occur.

"As you know, your family has kept a private apartment in this hotel as part of a 'residency in perpetuity' provision included in the original sale of the property. This provision has legally remained part of every additional sales agreement that the Mount Washington Hotel has undergone. Princess Carolyn Foster Stickney lived here for many years and your grandfather took up residency shortly after her death. Now with his passing, the residency falls to you as the last living heir to the Stickney fortune. I need to know—"

"I don't want it," I blurted out.

She looked at me for a moment before continuing. "I can appreciate why you feel that way, Darby, but it really isn't a choice you can make."

"I don't want to live in the hotel," I said honestly. "I'm not even sure I will be staying in Bretton Woods much longer."

"Be that as it may, you have responsibilities related to your family's estate. Whether you choose to remain here with us at the Mount Washington Hotel or not, the private apartment and all within it will remain yours," she said matter-of-factly. "I have already taken the liberty of moving your luggage out of your existing room on the third floor and into the antechamber of the apartment."

I thought about arguing the legalities of moving me against my will, but decided to leave it alone. Georgina was only doing what she was obligated to do. I didn't want to get her into any trouble.

"I'll make arrangements as soon as I can to pay for my original room."

"This is no need. A patron has already taken care of your expenses in full."

"What?" I was shocked. "Who paid my bill?"

"It doesn't matter who paid it. The patron insisted that they remain anonymous."

"Why...why would someone pay my bill?" I asked, searching for answers.

"Darby—" She paused, shaking her head and looking into my eyes, "—are you really so blind that you can't see the magnitude of what you have done? Did you not see what happened in that dining room here tonight? Complete strangers are drawn to you. They're proud of you. A hero like you doesn't come along every day."

"I'm no hero," I said, lowering my voice to a whisper.

"Well, I have a list of people four pages long who would disagree with you and because of them your money is no longer any good in my hotel. Whether you choose to stay or go, you will always have a place here, Darby...Stickney... Weeks," she said, emphasizing my middle name.

I exhaled, feeling a little dizzy and uncomfortable with the generosity being shown to me. The accolades being thrown at me were also misplaced. In the Navy, I was an observer of war and violence, but rarely an active participant in the fighting until that dreadful day. Why couldn't people just appreciate how well I took care of the men in my unit? I thought about the hypocrisy of war. If you kill someone in a time of war, they call you hero. But if you kill that same person at home in the name of vengeance, they lock you up. Where's the logic in that?

"Darby?" Georgina touched my arm, jolting me back to the present. "Are you OK?"

"I'm fine," I lied. "It's just a lot to process at one time."

"Why don't you go get some rest?" she said, handing me an ornate ebony box with the key to my future inside. "We'll chat again when you are up for it."

I sat for a few minutes after Georgina left, fingering the medal between my thumb and forefinger. I fled Bretton Woods to escape the heavy expectations. I returned drowning in unbearable admiration. I wasn't sure which one was worse.

Standing up, I wandered through the rest of the once-private dining room. On the opposite side of the room, two red-hooded chairs flanked a bone-white mantled fireplace, while to my right a draped sitting nook offered even more privacy. I thought about how many deals had been reached in this room over cocktails. Big money and big ideas crossed paths here, setting the stage for the Industrial Revolution and later the post-

World War II economic boom. For over a hundred years, this structure housed the elite of society and a Stickney had always been present, pulling strings and making things happen. What now?

Making my way to the door, I entered the Great Hall and headed for the elevator. As the doors opened, a young man with two prosthetic legs exited the lift. Upon seeing me, the man snapped to attention and rendered a crisp salute using a fabricated clear plastic hand. I returned the salute automatically, holding it longer than was required. Tears welled up in my eyes before streaming down my cheeks and soaking the starched collar of my shirt. The former marine dropped his salute and embraced me as I wept into his supportive shoulder. Comforting me, he whispered into my ear, "It's going to be all right." For the first time since returning to the North Country, I almost believed it.

CHAPTER 7

Pickford Marsh surveyed the valley of his ancestors under a cerulean blue sky. It had been ages since he last stood on top the windswept summit of the 'Rockpile'. Autumn had crept in early, weaving a patchwork of color across the landscape. To the west, smoke rose from one of Aqua-Nord's worksites. Pickford fumed; the ongoing treachery that plagued his operations was trying his patience. The felling of trees would recommence soon. Progress was at hand and he would not be denied.

"This is a waste of time," Dr. Young yelled out after he had finished collecting the last sample. "The geomorphology is all wrong, Mr. Marsh."

"I'm not paying you to chit chat, professor. We have another three sites to get to today," Pickford roared between clenched teeth, losing patience with his annoying employee.

"I think I know what I'm talking about, Mr. Marsh. I am a former Penrose Medal winner, you know. This whole cockamamie survey is not going to amount to anything."

"If you want your research money, doctor, I strongly suggest you get to work and stop badgering me. I'm sure I could find someone else who would just love their next five years of research funded in full."

If this gets out I'm going to be the laughingstock of the scientific community, Dr. Young thought to himself. *There is nothing of value up here or anywhere else in the North Country.*

***

Billowing smoke from the previous night's monkey wrenching was visible in the distance as the fog lifted. The rising sun revealed another blow to the armor of Aqua-Nord's teetering sense of invincibility. Pickford Marsh was incensed. He'd been on the phone already with the county sheriff, the state police, and finally the FBI. He wanted heads, either the arsonist's or the officials whose job it was to protect his interests. A command post was set up in the hotel's Gold Room as investigators were busy interviewing anyone who might have heard or seen anything remotely related to what they were calling an eco-terrorist attack. Pickford's money and influence got results.

"Catch any crooks yet?" I said, poking my head into the historic Gold Room.

Quinn Matthews paced the room, scanning the list of leads with indifference. This morning's round of interviews yielded mostly dead ends. With much dismay, he read Finnegan Doyle's name again off the list and tried to remain impartial. His training told him not to get emotionally involved, but hearing the

58

name of a former high school classmate from the mouth of an Aqua-Nord employee threw him for a loop. Quinn's former life as an FBI agent working out of the Boston field office had kept him far away from his boyhood home and the small town politics that went with it. Returning to the North Country thrust him unwittingly back into an antiquated land of petty gossip and moth-eaten grudges. I bet Quinn wished he was back in Boston right now, trudging through the Irish bars of Southie instead of tiptoeing through the blue blood minefield of Bretton Woods.

Looking up, Quinn smiled before responding to my question. "That depends...are you here to confess?"

"No, but I think Colonel Mustard did it in the Conservatory with his American Express Black Card."

Spitting out his coffee, Matthews admitted, "That's the most reasonable theory I've heard all morning. Sure tops the Sasquatch conspiracy Silas was mouthing off about earlier."

"Want to grab a fresh cup and walk a while?" I asked, hoping to catch up with my old friend.

"You bet." He grabbed his coat and sprinted from the room.

We exited onto the back veranda. An early season snow had frosted the peaks overnight, highlighting the cog railroad's path snaking up toward the summit. The beauty of the North County still took my breath away. Meandering back towards the South Porch, we helped ourselves to some coffee from one of the portable urns lining the deck and looked out at Mother Nature's beauty. The hanging planters framed a foursome as they played doubles on the clay tennis courts below us.

"Have they anointed you king yet?" Quinn teased.

Smirking, I answered, "No, but I do get free room and board."

"That sounds pretty good to me."

"Any time you want to trade lives," I said half kidding.

Quinn turned serious for a moment. "Is it really that bad?"

"I don't know," I sighed. "It's hard to explain." I stood up and moved closer to the railing. Gazing out at the Donald Ross designed golf course, I tried to change the subject. "It seems like ages ago that we caddied here, Quinn. Can you believe Silas actually asked me the other day if I was still hauling clubs?"

Quinn laughed. "Nothing that old kook says surprises me anymore. After talking to him, or should I say listening to him talk this morning, I think he's lost it. Maybe we can have him committed?"

"You were down in Boston for like, what, 15 years?"

Quinn paused for a minute before answering. "I really tried to make it up for the funeral, Darby, but—"

I raised my hand, cutting him off. I wasn't looking for an excuse from him. "It's OK. Neither one of us thought we'd ever come back here. The circumstances of our return is really mind boggling, don't you think?"

"Since you mentioned it, yes, it's definitely weird, but at least we can commiserate together."

"I heard that guy in the Gold Room mention Finnegan Doyle's name. Is he a suspect?" I asked, searching for some information.

"You know I can't talk about an ongoing investigation, Darby."

"The only reason I ask is because that's the second person I've heard mention Finn's name this week."

"What do you know?" Quinn asked quickly, switching back into head-of-security mode.

"I had dinner with Father Callaghan the other night."

Quinn rolled his eyes. "Another character I'm amazed is still alive. There's got to be something in the water up here that keeps these dinosaurs breathing."

"More like in the alcohol," I mused. "Father Callaghan was yapping to me about some eco-terror group—ELF, I think he said—and how Finnegan was mixed up with them out in Oregon."

"Interesting, but not very incriminating," Quinn replied. "I would say that our pal Finn is someone worth chatting with if given the chance, but no one is going to dedicate any of the assets needed to hunt him down at this point."

"I could try to find him," I said, surprising myself.

Quinn's expression turned suspicious. "You know where he is?"

"No, but I don't think that matters. He'll probably find me."

"Listen, Darby, if Finn really is involved with ELF then I can guarantee you he's much more dangerous now than he was in high school. He had plenty of reasons to want to kill you back then. What do you think is going to prevent him from putting a tree spike in your head now?"

"It all depends on whether he keeps childhood promises or not," I said cryptically.

"You wouldn't want to meet him out there in the woods, all by yourself," Quinn reminded me.

"You're probably right, but I don't have anything else to do," I said. "A little walk in the woods might do me some good."

"Just remember, that little medal isn't bulletproof, Darby. If you get yourself killed, your funeral is going to be one hell of a wicked pissah," he said jokingly in a strong Boston accent.

"Well then we should find a packie and celebrate before I go," I said, channeling my own Kennedy accent.

"I'm curious, Darby. Are you planning on staying in Bretton Woods for a while?"

"To tell you the truth, I haven't given it much thought yet. I don't really know what's next for me."

"Well, whatever you decide, I'm sure you'll have plenty of options. The whole country knows your name by now and you're the closest thing to a celebrity in Bretton Woods these days."

"I'm hardly a celebrity, Quinn."

"Oh yeah, what do you call that?" he said, pointing to the foursome now walking off of the clay tennis courts. Looking down, I spied the group of four middle-aged women who I didn't know waving and blowing kisses up to me as they walked towards the hotel.

"Maybe they have a thing for ex-FBI agents?" I said.

"I'm sure that's the reason," Quinn said with a laugh. "Keep telling yourself that, my friend, but sooner or later you'll have to face the truth."

At that moment, facing Finn sounded a hell of a lot safer than confronting the truth. I hoped I was right.

***

Einstein once wrote that coincidence is God's way of remaining anonymous. Emily's reappearance in my life was more than mere happenstance. She somehow knew I was there at the hotel. Our high-altitude tryst left me feeling dizzy and confused. I needed to clear my mind and release the tension building inside me. I retreated into the forests of my childhood.

I've always felt more at home in the woods. My senses come alive here with the smells of decaying wood and evergreen pine. In a verdant landscape, sounds are amplified and shadows are lengthened, exposing granite outcrops that hide the secrets of nature and men.

"Well…well…well," crooned a deep voice from the edge of the woods. "I must be dreaming."

My heart stopped and a chill accelerated up my spine as I turned to lay my eyes on another distant childhood memory. Peering out from the tree line, the intense gray eyes of Finnegan Doyle penetrated my calm exterior. How in the world did he sneak up on me?

"Damn, Finn, you scared the hell out of me," I replied a little too honestly.

"I seem to have that effect on people," he said with a quiet laugh. "What brings you way out here…all alone?" he added while sauntering towards me, closing the distance between us like a predatory cat.

I shrugged, collecting my thoughts and trying to get my nerves under control before answering him. "Is it true, Finn? Are you responsible for this?" I said, extending my arms and gesturing toward the rising smoke in the distance.

"Some would say that damn fool Pickford Marsh is responsible for his own troubles. He's destroying the beauty of these Great North Woods along with our homes and history, Darby. Many good people would like to stop Pickford. Why are you so quick to accuse me?"

"I've heard some talk around the hotel. Your name has come up more than once as a possible person of interest."

"Person of interest?" Finn howled, clearly amused. "You really should avoid people who speak in tongues and read lips. They could be bad for your health."

"Well, given your checkered history and your family name people unfortunately think the worst." I shrugged my shoulders again as I pulled out two Marlboros and put them in my mouth.

"Only you can prevent forest fires," Finn deadpanned as he ignited his Zippo, lighting the cigarettes and taking one from my mouth. "Things never do change, do they?" He took a deep drag. "Remember when we were kids? I was always the first one blamed when things went sour. Like that time with the broken light outside of old man Jolly's drug store. The sheriff came to my house first. He just knew I did it," Finn hissed with contempt in his voice. "You should have seen his face when he found out that you, the school valedictorian, were the vandal. Maybe you're the one messing with Pickford? Yeah, that would be classic."

I shook my head and laughed, avoiding Finn's eyes. After all these years, he still had a way of making me feel uneasy.

"I've got no beef with Pickford," I said. "Our issues are well in the past. I do, however, have a beef with anyone who hurts innocent people. Those construction workers are just doing a job. It allows them to feed their families and put a roof over their heads. They shouldn't have to fear for their lives because some fool spikes a tree or booby-traps their equipment. They need to be protected."

"And who protects the trees that get cut down?" Finn responded. "What about the whitetail deer, the moose, the black bear, the eagle, or even the catamount? What about their rights and homes? Who stands up for them?"

"They're not people, Finn," I scoffed, becoming annoyed. "They're wild animals. They'll move on to other areas or die."

"The U.S. government thought the same thing about the Abenaki and the Mohawk," Finn countered.

I closed my eyes and exhaled a long drag of cigarette smoke. I had quit smoking years ago, but found myself craving the nicotine again since stepping back into the North Country. I knew Finn was trying to provoke me on purpose and I wasn't going to win a debate against him. My cigarette was barely keeping my blood pressure under control. "You and I are very different people, Finn. You put a higher value on the natural world than I do. The point is I've seen enough pain and death. I don't want to see any more. People will die for the most meaningless things in the world, but those very same people somehow can never manage to find happiness or beauty in the things living right in front of them. The lines between civilization and savagery are often blurred, but violence is never the answer."

Finn stood silently for a minute, taking in the vista. "You and I are more alike than you think. We've both outgrown this little northern town, and yet we both seem to find a way back here when the outside world gets overly complicated."

"That might be true," I admitted, "but at least I've done something positive with my life since leaving. I've made a difference."

Finn looked me straight in the eyes. "Yeah, I read about your bullshit heroics. They pinned a big-ass shiny medal on your chest, thanked you for your service, then kicked your ass out the door. I imagine most people would feel downright euphoric about that, but if I had to guess, I would think it just made you feel plain uncomfortable, didn't it? So with nowhere else to go you come running home to the open arms of Bretton Woods.

65

How's it feel, Darby? Did it make it all better? Are you clean again?"

"We're nothing alike," I said, shaking my head. "You hide way out here, cut off from people living your Deep Ecology bullshit, then you hurt innocent people when they don't agree with your worldview. That's noble, Finn."

"You can lecture me all you want about good and evil, but you can't run from your problems, and this problem—" Finn said, pointing to himself, "—won't run from Pickford Marsh, you, or anyone else. My advice to you is to be very careful when choosing sides. Things are not always as they seem. Small towns can harbor big problems."

"Just don't hurt anyone else and we'll be fine."

Finn took another long drag. "So you've never killed anyone?" he asked, pushing just the right buttons.

My eyes fell to the ground as he continued to speak. Dark distorted visions of blood and cratered landscapes filled my mind. I could smell the charred flesh again and I could hear the cries of the dying. I saw my friends being pulled away by a shadowy enemy. I dropped my med pack, chambered a rifle, and shot them all dead. The healer had become a hunter.

"Twelve years in the tribal lands of Afghanistan and Iraq and you never wanted to kill anyone? Who you kidding, Darby?" he said with a chuckle.

Trying to calm the anger that was rising within me, I began to utter between clenched teeth. "My job was to watch out for the Marines in my care, to heal them when they got hurt. Whether or not I shot a weapon is irrelevant—"

"Bullshit! It's completely relevant," he shouted back at me. "You unexpectedly appear after being away some twenty-odd years and you have the gall to come way out here and preach to me about morality? You know nothing about me or anyone else who's left in this broken town. I'm just someone you used to know. I've grown up. I've moved on. I'm not who I was twenty years ago, Darby, so don't judge me based on your faded memories of who I was at seventeen."

"Great speech, Finn, but it doesn't change the fact that although we're physically different people today, our character doesn't change. The biggest difference between us is that I did something you never could do. You can't even fathom the idea in that miniscule brain of yours. You monkey-wrench equipment, you hurt people, and worst of all you do it to protect a damn…what? Squirrel? Hurting people is the most primitive and easiest thing in the world to do. If you really want to challenge yourself, if you really want to test your mettle, if you really want to win your drunk-ass step-daddy's elusive approval then why don't you try doing the hardest thing imaginable? Try healing someone for a change."

Finn pulled out a hunting knife, lunged at me and pressed it against my throat. Our eyes locked. I was no longer held captive by his youthful fundamentalism. Finn's eyes betrayed the newfound fear that coursed through his veins. I slowly twisted free from Finn's grip, turning my back on him and extinguishing my cigarette beneath my boot. I took a few steps down the trail, back toward the safety of the hotel, before turning around again, intent on asking Finn one last question. But he was gone. Gone like the elusive catamount, a ghost struggling to protect its once vast kingdom in the vanishing wilds of the Great North Woods.

CHAPTER 8

Jacques Robarge looked into his bathroom mirror and examined a face that he no longer recognized. His time in America had been lucrative, but being the public face of Aqua-Nord was a thankless job made worse by the incessant demands of his employer, Pickford Marsh.

The lines around his hard eyes betrayed his age. It was difficult being alone and French. Jacques removed a Gauloises Carporal cigarette from its baby blue pack and placed it in his mouth. There were many things he loved about being in America, but its weak cigarettes were revolting. He flipped his lighter and ignited the butt, taking a long drag. He felt a wave of relaxation settle over him as the nicotine entered his bloodstream. A virile mood settled in as he thought about tonight's soirée. It had been far too long since he last explored the touch, taste, and smell of a woman. Giselle's call had been quite unexpected, but filled him with glorious anticipation. She caught his eye during a company gathering when he first arrived from Marseille. She undressed him with her wicked eyes and radiated a powerful sexuality that enticed him. *Tonight I will finally have her*, he thought to himself as the cold straight-edged razor slid across his stubbled face.

Jacques recalculated his plan as he finished shaving and splashed the remnants of his Hugo Boss Cotton & Verbena cologne on his face and chest. He had originally planned on flying home tonight, but Giselle's invitation forced him to change his timetable. He would now thoroughly enjoy himself tonight. In the morning he would tender his resignation from Aqua-Nord effective immediately and then make the long drive to Logan International Airport and hop on an evening flight to Paris. He'd be having lunch within sight of the wild flamingos at the Plage de l'Almanarre in Hyères within two days. He could hardly wait to say *au revoir* to his ulcer-inducing position and the cantankerous Pickford Marsh.

Jacques smiled for the first time in months as he thought about the look on his boss's face when he realized his point man on the Granite Pass Project was gone. Even though he was still under contract, what could the Aqua-Nord do to him? If they try suing him, he'll just threaten to divulge all the bribes and illegal arm-twisting that was occurring in an effort to get the land rights for the transmission lines. Pickford Marsh would soon learn that he wasn't the only one who could play hardball.

"*Va te faire foutre!*" he shouted out loud. Go fuck yourself!

***

Giselle was the ultimate fixer of things, a cleaner for those who could pay. After receiving Pickford Marsh's call, she began to prepare the toxic treat. Ethylene glycol was her poison of choice. Its sweet taste could be mixed with just about any food or drink. She had used it hundreds of times with deadly precision. It was readily available and could be bought at any gas station or hardware store without drawing even the slightest suspicion or raised eyebrow.

The gelatinous, antifreeze-laced dessert would be the assassin tonight. She chose a strawberry flavor knowing it was her victim's favorite. With any luck, she would be a hundred miles away when the ingested venom worked its magic. He would feel intoxicated at first, unable to focus or see straight. Then he would start to vomit. His blood would grow acidic, causing his kidneys to fail. Death would be painful. Pickford's men would then dispose of the body like all the others in the past. The lifeless figure would just vanish into the wilderness, ceasing to exist. It was easy money for her.

Giselle picked up the phone and made the call. He could not wait to see her. *Men, so easily deceived.* All you need to do is hint at the possibility of sex and they will do whatever you ask - fools!

***

Jacques Robarge was to rendezvous with Giselle at the hotel's annual Great Gatsby weekend celebration. As he waited for her arrival, he perused the massive beer offerings of the temporary beer garden set up on the resort's clay tennis courts and was thrilled to find a Belgian Pale Ale called *The French Connection.*

Pouring the hazy blonde beer into his glass stein, Jacques took a swig and thought about the freedom that awaited him on tomorrow's flight home. For the past eleven years, he had toiled for Aqua-Nord, climbing the corporate ladder to become one of

Pickford Marsh's right-hand men. He was a results man who Pickford entrusted with the toughest assignments. Jacques initially enjoyed the challenges, doing whatever it took to meet the objective. He never failed so leaving now was, in a sense, admitting defeat for the first time in his life. However, it was the right thing to do.

Pickford Marsh was obsessed with the Granite Pass Project. Pickford could care less about hydroelectric clean energy or the jobs propaganda that was being spewed in the public forums. He wanted the gross easements over the land. Aqua-Nord's power transmission lines would be the first phase of a multi-phase plan. The crowning jewel would be the completion of a tar sands pipeline snaking hundreds of miles through the North Country. It would bring the bituminous sands from the frozen Canadian oil fields to Portland, Maine. The harbor was a critical exit point and a new pipeline was necessary to move the roughly 170 billion proven barrels to market. The profits for Aqua-Nord would be astronomical. Pickford would say and do anything to see its completion.

Jacques had grown wary of a plan that had repeatedly encountered roadblock after roadblock. City councils in every northern town, village, and hamlet had dragged their feet. Protests were staged and moratoriums were passed. The writing was on the wall, but Pickford Marsh refused to concede defeat. He pushed harder and his strong-arm tactics had become ever more distasteful to Jacques. It was time to wash his hands of the whole mess and get out while there was still time. Tomorrow was a new day.

The crowd had begun to grow larger as the sun set and the darkness set in. Jacques wandered further down towards the gently flowing Ammonoosuc River that ran through the hotel grounds. Giselle had instructed him to meet her by the river. She was late, his beer was empty, and he was growing increasingly hungry. As luck would have it, a hotel banquet waiter passed him heading in the opposite direction with hors d'oeuvres. Jacques grabbed a skewer of chicken and downed a glass of strawberry Jell-O shots. He normally didn't like to mix his alcohols, but he couldn't resist his favorite sweet treat.

Reaching the water's edge, he was greeted by the soothing sounds of the night. The water lapped at the shore, filling him with a sense of calm that he hadn't felt in years. The alcohol was stronger than he had expected. His vision began to blur and it was hard to focus. He castigated himself for getting drunk before Giselle had even arrived. He wanted to remember the conquest that her body would offer tonight, but he was feeling increasingly ill. Doubling over, he puked into the water as cold sweats erupted all over him. His breathing grew labored and his vision dimmed. Taking one last deep breath, darkness filled his eyes as he fell forward into the cold waters of the river below.

Jacques Robarge was finally free.

***

Father Callaghan enjoyed his routine evening walks from the hotel to the chapel when the weather was mild and the skies were clear like tonight. It allowed him to gaze into the heavens and observe the constellations, something he did often in his youth during his dark days in Vietnam. It had been forty plus years since he was last in-country, but the brutality and pointless deaths fought over meaningless mounds of dirt remained fresh in his mind. Oh how he had changed since his greenhorn days as a Navy chaplain. The recent local violence had caused him to remember things that should have remained dead and buried in the jungles of Southeast Asia. He coped with the memories by drowning them in a monsoon of liquor.

Tonight's themed weekend made the hotel's grounds too crowded for Father Callaghan's liking. He struggled to navigate the normal pathways, bumping and staggering into costumed Roarin' 20s couples and Guilded Age bachelors. Crowds made him uneasy nowadays so he detoured down to the river. Removing his shoes, he entered the Ammonoosuc. The cold rush of the water shocked his body, clearing his head of the effects of too many dinner cocktails. He followed the serpentine waterway downstream, leaving the hotel behind. He decided to ford the stream and cross over to the chapel once he passed the golf course's clubhouse.

The evening sounds of summer had waned with the changing seasons and were replaced by an autumn stillness now only interrupted by the bubbling river. The water numbed his feet but invigorated his body. It took extreme sensations to make Callaghan's aged body feel alive nowadays. He couldn't wait to finally retire and move someplace warm like Costa Rica or St. Lucia. He could live his remaining days in comfort and isolation. *Just one more winter,* he told himself.

The sound of unnatural splashes ahead interrupted his feeling of relaxation. As he looked further downstream, he could just make out the silhouettes of two people bending down into the water. He hoped it wasn't another couple skinny-dipping in the darkness of an early autumn night. He was in no condition to deliver another lecture on modesty and decency. Continuing to walk downstream, he realized there were not two, but three people in the water. The third person was being lifted out of the river by the other two. They were struggling with the task.

73

"Are you all right? Do you need any help?" Father Callaghan called as he clicked on his flashlight and continued to move closer to the group.

The sound of a person falling back into the river alerted Callaghan that something was not quite right as two men moved rapidly upstream toward him. His instincts told him to retreat toward the opposite shore and try to put space between him and his pursuers. Then, without warning, a sharp object pierced his leg as he exited the water. The pain was immense, but he kept moving towards the trees. *If I can just get to the safety of the chapel*, he told himself. His adrenaline kicked in as he plowed through the undergrowth and emerged into the open lot of the church. His vision blurred as he pushed open the sanctuary doors and collapsed onto the cobblestone floor. His hands trembled as they searched the floor for a place to hide the knowledge he carried in his pocket. Footsteps echoed nearby as hands began to touch him. He lost consciousness, already prepared to meet his maker.

CHAPTER 9

The scarred dirt path had become overgrown with knee-high grass that danced in the early autumn wind. Two deep, well-worn wheel ruts lay hidden beneath Mother Nature's incursion. Extending my hand, I chopped at the weeds as I meandered up toward the seasonal chapel. How many times had I played on these grounds as a child? The site looked exactly as I remembered it. Although just a stone's throw from Route 302, the Episcopalian chapel had an isolated and remote feel to it, precisely how the princess had envisioned it.

I always thought of the Stickney Chapel as a mini castle with its gray granite stone turret and blood-red door. The rest of the world knew it as the Church of the Transfiguration, but for me it was always a fortress of solitude. I could shut the world out here and talk to my father. I would tell him about my life and wonder about his. Why did he leave me so unprepared?

Entering the chapel, I was greeted by the Twelve Apostles, witnesses to a second killing of a holy man. Police tape still blocked off the place of desecration. A stain was still visible where the blood had pooled in front of the holy alter.

Twelve Tiffany stained-glass windows, each representing one of Jesus' followers, radiated light into the sanctuary as I walked down the cobbled center aisle and took a seat in the front oak pew. My eyes took in the images of the Transfiguration hovering above the alter. It recounted the moment when Jesus became radiant upon the mountain, the point of intersection between man and the heavens.

"Death is rarely pleasant," a voice echoed behind me, shattering the silence.

Turning my head, I eyed Quinn standing in the doorway. "Do the local authorities have any leads?"

"Nope. Nobody saw or heard anything. Best we can tell, the death occurred sometime between 9:00 PM and midnight. Hard to tell when there's no body."

"Any chance it's not Father Callaghan?" I asked. Of course I hoped he was still alive, but I remembered our last conversation. He told me something was brewing, that he had this sense of dread reminiscent of how he felt in Vietnam. *If I die, seek out the knowledge, follow the riddles,* he'd said. Not one to sit idly by, I'd have to work the riddles to see if they contained the information my family had entrusted to Callaghan.

"The local sheriff has jurisdiction at the moment. It's not an FBI case—yet—but no one can recall seeing Father Callaghan since you ate dinner with him the other night."

I nodded my head, understanding the implication of those words. "So I'm the last person who remembers seeing him alive? I assume the sheriff will want to ask me some questions?"

"Actually, the sheriff asked me to handle the interview since you and I are old friends." Quinn walked down the aisle and took a seat in the pew behind me. "Can you tell me about your encounter with Father Callaghan the other night?"

"I was supposed to meet someone else for dinner and showed up a little early. I didn't want to wait in the bar, so I asked Flavio if anyone was eating alone who I might be able to join while I waited. Flavio seated me with Callaghan. He was already drunk by the time I got there."

"Who were you supposed to meet?" Quinn asked.

"Emily Baines."

"Oh man, how did that go?" he said, already knowing the answer.

"She stood me up."

"Jesus," he said with a laugh. "Things never do change do they, Darby?"

"Guess not," was all I could manage to say.

"What did you and Father Callaghan talk about?"

"Callaghan was pissed off with all the recent violence that was happening around town. It was having a negative impact on church attendance and he wasn't very happy about it. He said the senseless violence reminded him of Vietnam and that he was worried."

"What was he worried about?" Quinn pressed.

"I don't really know. He mentioned that someone broke into the Rectory and ransacked the place. The police downplayed the incident saying it was probably just local kids getting their jollies on a Friday night. He wanted to show me something he thought whoever broke into the church might have been after."

"Did he mention what it was?"

"He said it was related to my family. He thought it might help me answer some questions I had about my past. He was really drunk, Quinn, and making no sense."

Quinn processed this information as he rose out of the pew and moved so that he was standing over the blood-stained floor. "Assuming that Father Callaghan is dead, it would appear he was first attacked somewhere outside of the chapel. There's a blood trail leading up from the river indicating he most likely fled into the sanctuary before expiring at the foot of the alter."

"Where's his body then?" I asked.

"It had to have been removed by the killer…or killers. The absence of a body complicates the investigation and makes it more difficult to figure out what happened here. All we have is a bunch of blood which the medical examiner is testing to see if it's indeed Father Callaghan's or not."

"So we just wait and do nothing in the meantime?"

"No, we pursue other leads, Darby."

"What other leads?" I asked.

"Do you happen to know if this chapel used to have ivy growing on it?" Quinn asked in a serious tone.

Confused by the randomness of his question, I thought about it for a minute before answering, "Yeah, I think so. When I was younger, I seem to remember seeing an old black and white postcard of the chapel in my grandfather's room. Ivy was scaling up one of the exterior walls. How did you know that?"

"Just a guess related to this," he said, handing me a faded scrap of folded up parchment. "We found this hidden in a crack in the floor near the pool of blood. I think Father Callaghan may have hid it there before meeting his final end."

"Why would he hide this?" I asked, eyeing the parchment.

"Probably to protect it. I think Callaghan didn't want his killer to find it."

"He was killed over a poem?" I said, unfolding the paper and reading the inscription.

"The county sheriff has already dismissed that theory, saying anyone could have stuck the paper in the crack given how old it looks. The sheriff is pursuing a simple robbery motive."

"Was anything stolen from the chapel?" I asked.

"Not that I can see," Quinn said, looking around the chapel.

"Then why does the sheriff think this is a robbery case?"

"Good question," Quinn replied. "The sheriff took a phone call while I was here with him. I heard a lot of shouting from whomever he was talking to on the other end of his cell phone. He became pretty tight-lipped after hanging up which made me a little suspicious. So I did some investigating of my own. I called a few of my old contacts at the Bureau. Guess who the sheriff moonlights for on the side?"

"Aqua-Nord?" I guessed, knowing how many public officials were already wrapped around the North Country's biggest employer.

"Bingo," Quinn said, pointing at me.

"You think Pickford Marsh is involved in this?" I asked.

"If he is, I'm going to find out. Nothing would give me more pleasure than taking down Pickford Marsh."

I looked at the poem again and read it out loud.

Where the ivy used to grow,
Knowledge is now stowed.
Find the rock star not boulder,
And a sweet tooth's fix holder.
The truth is hiding in the cracks.

"What does it mean?" I asked.

"I was hoping you could tell me, Darby"

I read the poem several more times, looking for something familiar, but my mind was empty. I hated riddles and had little patience for them. "I don't know," I said. "I didn't major in English Lit. It's all gibberish to me."

"Think. It might help Father Callaghan," Quinn said, trying to motivate me. "If the chapel is the place where the ivy used to grow then who's the rock star and what's a sweet tooth's fix holder?"

My mind was still swirling from all the alcohol I had consumed over the past few days making it hard for me to focus. I hadn't been in this chapel for almost twenty years. As a kid, I mostly played outside on the grounds, pretending to lay seize to the castle and scale its granite rock walls. *"Find the rock star not boulder,"* I repeated, thinking of my youth. "Look at the spelling of boulder, Quinn."

"What about it?" he asked.

"There's no musical rock stars in Bretton Woods, but there are plenty of granite stones," I reminded him.

"I still don't get it," Quinn admitted.

"The riddle is referring not to a person who's a rock star, but to a stone with a star embedded in it!"

"Are you sure?" Quinn asked.

"Absolutely…and I know where to find it too. Follow me."

Exiting the protection of the sanctuary, Quinn and I burst into the bright sunshine of a perfect Indian summer day. The temperatures were unseasonably warm for the fall causing a quick sweat to break out on my face as I sprinted to the front of the chapel closest to the road. I knew it was here somewhere. I remembered seeing it through my child-aged eyes. I scanned the rock facade of the church looking for the star-inscribed stone. Quinn joined me once he realized what I was doing and began working from the opposite corner. I touched each stone as I checked it, reaching as high as my arms would stretch. After a couple of minutes, Quinn and I met in the middle. Neither one of us had found the stone.

"Maybe it's higher up?" Quinn suggested.

"No, I clearly remember being able to see it from the ground when I was a kid. Let's split up and check the other sides of the chapel," I suggested.

Quinn headed to the east side while I decided to examine the exterior back wall of the chapel. Using the same search method as before, I worked my way across the north-facing wall touching the individual stones. As I neared the northwest corner, I began to lose hope. Maybe my memory had failed me…and then I saw it. Nestled in the stone support column, I saw the rock star. The slanted five-pointed figure was implanted in an orange-brown felsic rock high on the column. I shouted for Quinn who arrived in a flash.

"Now that is definitely a rock star," he said, smiling from ear to ear.

"Give me a lift so I can get a closer look," I commanded.

Locking his fingers together, Quinn hoisted me up. The decorative star was truly impressive up close. *The truth is hiding in the cracks.* I noticed that the grout at the base of the star had been removed, leaving a deep pocket between the rocks. Unfolding my pocketknife, I probed the space and removed a thin metal container that was about the size of a business card holder.

"What did you find?" Quinn shouted up to me.

"Lower me down and I'll show you." Reaching the ground, I examined the thin golden case, twirling it around in my hand. "It's heavy for its size."

"It's made of real gold," Quinn observed. "Open it up."

Lifting the lid, I was surprised to find another piece of faded parchment inside. Unfolding it, I realized it was another riddle. I read it out loud.

With a drizzly November in my soul,
Behind a Michael Smalle penned letter is foretold,
The heir to the king of coal marks the view in which you seek
In Concord, the silhouette and bones, the perfect gleek.

"Well that clears things up," I said in jest.

"Riddles upon more riddles," Quinn lamented, handing me another golden case.

"Where did you get this?" I asked, surprised to see a matching case.

"Follow me and I'll show you," he said as he walked backed toward the east wall   of the chapel. "I'll give you *a sweet tooth's fix holder.*"

Turning the corner, I was enlightened. Plastered into another rock support column, two feet off the ground, was the image of a decorative granite ice cream cone. Slanted like the rock star, a discolored stone to the right of cone had already been removed.

"I found the case behind the stone," Quinn explained. "Open it up."

Lifting the lid of the second golden case revealed yet another piece of parchment. Unfolding the paper, I read the third riddle out loud.

> *Follow the Catamount and Bear oblique*
> *To uncover the past, the truth will reek.*
> *The pit of hell, a well of lost souls*
> *Justice be swift, the names extolled.*

I shook my head, not knowing what to think. "We solved one riddle only to uncover two more."

"Welcome to my world," Quinn said with a smile. "This is what investigators do every day, except we rarely encounter cryptic riddles written on parchment and hidden behind stones."

"Can I keep these for a little bit?" I asked, holding the two cases in my hands.

"Since it's not an FBI case and the idiot sheriff doesn't think it makes for relevant crime scene evidence, be my guest, but I'm curious what you're going to do with them?"

"I plan to do a little digging of my own," I said, thinking of one person who might be able to help decipher all these riddles. I just didn't know if I could bring myself to face him.

***

Pickford Marsh's office smelled like an amalgamation of formaldehyde and whiskey. The pungency of the stench was heightened exponentially by the murkiness of the musty room.

An impenetrable barrier of curtains had shut out all natural light which instilled a sense of dread in me as I sat down in a grotesquely expensive Eileen Gray Dragon chair and waited for the arrival of my childhood fear.

His entrance was stealthy and swift. He flowed into the room like mustard gas, taking a seat on a perch behind a hand-carved mahogany desk.

"The prodigal son returns," he said while swirling cubes of ice in a highball glass. "To what do I owe the honor of your presence, Master Weeks?"

"I've come to discuss a truce between our two families," I said, steadying my nerves.

"A truce! Now isn't that grand," he replied between clenched teeth. "You're a little late to the party, don't you think? Why would I want to entertain a truce with you?"

"Our two families once reaped massive rewards tied to their partnership to the developed North Country. Unfortunately, it fell apart long ago after a falling out of—"

"A falling out? Is that what you call it?" Pickford said with evil eyes, interrupting me as he leaned down from his elevated chair. "It was more like a casting out, an expulsion from society. Joseph Stickney humiliated my family which resulted in a century of anguish and misfortune."

"The actions of the Marsh family caused your century of anguish, but I doubt there was any financial misfortune considering the chair I'm sitting in, Mr. Marsh. My family just had the means and guts to carry out the sentence for your relatives' crimes."

"Crimes? You mean indiscretions," Pickford said with an air of innocence.

84

"Rape is not a gaffe nor a folly. It's repugnant and vile. What happened to your family was self-imposed by the actions of your own grandfather," I said. I felt sick to be in the presence of such arrogance.

"Nobody was raped. The women in question enjoyed themselves quite thoroughly, I'm sure. They were all well cared for and pampered before, during, and after copulation. They just got greedy and wanted more than they were worth."

"So they deserved to have their necks cut and their bodies dumped into the wilderness?"

"Never proven. No bodies were ever found," Pickford said with a smile. "For all we know, those women left Bretton Woods on their own free will and shacked up with other men somewhere else. It's all ancient history anyway."

"Then why not bury the hatchet and call a truce between our two families?" I repeated.

"Last time I looked, your family consisted of only one remaining blood relative – YOU. Why would I make peace when I can snuff out the bloodline permanently?"

"Are you threatening me, Mr. Marsh?"

"Of course not, I'm just thinking out loud," he said, burning a hole through me with his eyes. "Don't worry. You're probably more likely to suffer an accident like your grandfather or your cowardly father. I'll outlive you, your family, and that damn hotel. So if I were you, I'd give some serious thought about leaving Bretton Woods while you are still in…good health. You're good at running away and hiding, now aren't you boy?"

I felt my fists clench and my blood pressure rise. If it weren't for his two goons standing sentry over him, I would snap his little neck like a wishbone and avenge the deaths of my brood.

"You scared me as a young child, Mr. Marsh," I said after taking several deep breaths, "but I'm all grown up now. I was in fact considering leaving Bretton Woods, but you just gave me the biggest reason to stay. I'm going to find out the truth about your family and mine. We'll see what skeletons you have hiding in your closet."

Pickford smiled at me, revealing a crooked mouth full of burnt okra-colored teeth. "Your father once sat in that very same seat you now occupy and told me the exact same thing. Now look what happened to him. You will lose, Darby Weeks, and when you do, Joseph Stickney's seed will finally be snuffed out."

I stood up and walked toward the door fuming, but determined to keep my head. I wouldn't let Pickford incite me. There would be another time and place to avenge what was lost. He would not win.

"Before you go, Master Weeks, can I interest you in some strawberry Jell-O?" he said with a cackle.

***

The handwritten stanzas scribed on the yellowed parchment consumed my thoughts. Was this what Father Callaghan wanted to show me? If it was, how did it relate to my family? A bevy of questions swarmed in my head. The lack of real answers deepened my frustration and caused me to consider options that ranged from horrible to certifiably insane. I decided that I was in the dubious position of needing Silas Bollerud's assistance. *I'm so going to regret this.*

"So let me get this straight," Silas trumpeted as he navigated the hotel's buffet lunch offerings, "you're at an impasse and require the assistance of my inexhaustible pool of knowledge?"

"Yes," I groveled, "I believe you are the only one capable of shedding some light on something I found."

"Glorious!" he roared, scooping up an extra helping of Tandoori Chicken and placing it on his plate next to a towering mound of Basmati rice pilaf. "Then sit with me and we can discuss the nature of your predicament."

Following Silas outside to a sunny al fresco patio table, I stopped in my tracks when I discovered he already had a lunchtime companion.

"Darby Weeks, I believe you already know Ms. Emily Baines."

"Hello, my love," she said in an alluring voice.

"Silas, maybe we can talk another time when you're alone?"

"'Fraid not," he said with a mouth full of rice. "I'm terribly busy and rarely alone. Speak now or forever hold your peace."

"Hmm…how I've always longed to hear those words," Emily cooed.

Releasing the mother of all sighs, I reluctantly sat down and ordered the largest draft beer available. If I was to endure this humiliation, I wasn't going to do it sober.

"I suppose you heard about the murder at the chapel," I said.

"Yes, a heinous and cowardly crime. I hope they catch the perpetrator and exact a pound of flesh in vengeance," Silas snorted.

"Me too," Emily added. "Father Callaghan was a little rough along the edges, but inside he was a decent man."

"I spoke to him the other night at dinner…after being stood up," I said, glaring at Emily who flashed me a look of innocence before sticking her tongue out at me. "Callaghan wanted me to come see him today. He said he had something related to my family that he wanted to show me."

"What was it?" Emily said with renewed interest.

"This." I placed one of the folded-up pieces of paper between them. Silas lifted the parchment and unfolded it with a gentleness normally reserved for unexploded ordinance.

"A poem?" Emily stated, glancing over Silas' shoulder.

"A quatrain, to be exact," Silas declared. "Did you know that the quatrain can be found in the poetic traditions of all the great ancient civilizations? The Chinese, the Romans, and the Greeks? The Greeks were especially skilled in this art form. In fact—"

Oh my god, what have I unleashed? I thought, drowning out Silas' verbal assault with my newly arrived beer. *This was a very bad idea.*

"—there are twelve distinct rhyming schemes associated with a quatrain, but I tend to be partial to the heroic stanza of ABAB. Simpletons like yourself, Darby, might recognize it by its vulgar peasant name – iambic pentameter."

"You really know how to excite a lady, Silas," Emily quipped.

"Well, I should. I've been married five times, six if you count that time in the Kalahari Desert when I unwittingly participated in a Saan wedding ritual. At the time I wasn't that familiar with the Khoisan languages of Southern Africa. I was mimicking the natives' use of their click consonants and before I knew it, I was the new son-in-law of the chief. I still have the caracal wedding stole. Best wedding gift I ever received. That reminds me, I once had a violin teacher who told me that

88

'marriage is indeed grand; divorces, a hundred grand.' Boy, was he ever right."

"If you don't mind, can we get back to my situation?" I asked.

"Ah yes, the poem." Silas studied it closely for a minute, then read it out loud at Emily's urging.

> *With a drizzly November in my soul,*
> *Behind a Michael Smalle penned letter is foretold,*
> *The heir to the king of coal marks the view in which you seek*
> *In Concord, the silhouette and bones, the perfect gleek.*

"Not the most euphonious language, mind you, but still intriguing," Silas announced. "It might sound better in the Khoisan tongue. Would you like to hear—?"

"No!" Emily and I said in unison.

"Bloody peasants," Silas scoffed before returning his gaze to the poem. "When faced with a riddle, I always find it best to take it one line at a time since every journey begins with a single step. For our first step, we will need to embark on a grand journey and leave Bretton Woods for a time. While I am an expert on many things, we will require the special skills of another. Are you willing to do this in an effort to gain the knowledge we will need?"

"Yes," Emily and I said in unison again.

"Now wait a minute," I said, looking at Emily, "I came to Silas alone for assistance. This is none of your concern."

Silas cut in. "Unfortunately, Darby, I believe we will require Ms. Baines' assistance at some point. We cannot make this journey without her."

"See, somebody's smart enough to appreciate me," Emily said with a smirk.

"His eyesight is just so poor he can't see right through you like I can," I said.

"While I can appreciate the importance of the ongoing courtship ritual that is occurring between the two of you since it kind of reminds me of the frigate bird's inflatable giant red throat sac, we are wasting time and I need to make a few phone calls posthaste in order to shed some additional light on your riddle. I'll let you know what I find out."

"Thank you, Silas," I said. "By the way, we definitely are not courting."

"Keep telling yourself that, young man, and maybe someone we will actually believe you. Now scat, and let me do what I do best."

This is without a doubt a huge mistake.

CHAPTER 10

I opened the ebony box and stared at the antique key to the private apartment. It looked like something you would expect to find in a medieval castle. It was aged bronze and heavily pitted. The key's bow was bell-like in shape with an orate 'S' scrolled inside it. Standing in the antechamber of the apartment, I inserted the bit into the lock and turned the key; a loud click greeted me. I put my shoulder up against the door and shoved. It took considerable effort to push the solid oak door open due to the sheer heft of the wood and the multitude of memories pushing back at me.

Crossing over the threshold, I stepped into the most exclusive and private time capsule. The wealth permeating from the main gathering room was staggering. Although I had lived here in my youth, it still took my breath away. Dominating the room was a massive twelve-foot high Badminton Cabinet. Crafted in Florence during the Medici reign, it was a magnificent piece. Its existence was unknown outside of this room and a closely guarded family secret. Its twin, incorrectly believed to be the only one in the world, had sold for over thirty million dollars at auction. Its dark ebony wood was inlaid with precious stones, a technique I remember my grandfather called *Pietre dure*. On the opposite wall stood two Goddard & Townsend Chippendale antique secretary desks and a Harrington Commode. The whole room was a treasure chest filled with numerous Germain Royal Soup Tureens, Scandinavian Battle Horns, and Japanese Porcelain Moon Flasks. It was an auctioneer's wet dream, but a reoccurring nightmare for me. I could never fathom how anyone in good conscience could possess a hundred-million-dollar room trapped inside a one-million-dollar hotel, and now it was all mine.

My ringing cell phone jolted me back to the present.

"Hey Darby, what'cha doing?" cooed Emily.

"Balancing my checkbook," I said without a thought.

"Did you get my note the other night? I got tied up with work and couldn't leave. I hope you didn't eat alone?"

"Don't worry, I wasn't lonely."

"I wanted to make it up to you. Are you free for dinner tonight? I'm buying."

"Listen, Emily, I'm dealing with some family issues today. Maybe some other time," I said unconvincingly.

"Awww...don't be that way. Is this because you think I stood you up?" she asked. "I just told you, I had a problem at work that required my full attention. If you meet me tonight, I'll make it worth your while," she purred, tempting me in a way only she could do.

I paused for a moment, hearing that voice in my head telling me to run far, far away. *Screw it.* I jumped back into the hot mess again. "When and where, Emily?"

"Meet me on the lower level of the hotel at Stickney's Restaurant around seven. I reserved the best table in the house with a mountain sunset view."

"You sure you wouldn't want to go someplace outside of the hotel? Like Fabyan's perhaps?"

"How blue collar of you. Do you have a coupon or something?" she said with a laugh.

"No, I just like the place. It's family friendly and not pretentious. I also really like their fried green tomato sandwiches."

"Oh Darby, don't make me laugh. Stickney's at 7 o'clock sharp," she said, then the line went dead.

Damn pushy New Yorkers. Why do I continue to let her boss me around?

***

Located just below the grand lobby of the Mount Washington Hotel, Stickney's Way bustled with life. The long thoroughfare connected the resort's post office to the indoor pool. Along the way, a game room, gift shop, and even a Starbucks offered guests more places to spend their hard-earned vacation money. Ironically, I was sure that my great grandfather's original vision for the wealthy retreat didn't contain such pedestrian distractions. Nestled among these sundry shops, The Cave and Stickney's Restaurant offered a loftier class of diversion at a higher price as well.

I checked in with the hostess and was shown to my seat by the back window. Although I had arrived exactly at 7:00 pm,

Emily was not waiting for me. *I swear to God, if she stands me up again…*

"Darby S. Weeks, are you following me?" chirped the voice of annoyance.

Not if you were the last human being alive. Looking to my right, I spied Silas sitting at the table next to mine, picking at his food.

"Just grabbing a bite to eat, Silas. What looks good on the menu tonight?"

"Well, I started with the seared crab cakes with caper rémoulade, but I took one bite and had to send it back. The sauce was so amateurish I'm sure the chef must be using Miracle Whip for the base. Next I made the awful mistake of trying the vegetable tofu Napoleon. Once you eat it, you'll have to definitely water the loo yourself."

Ugh.

"Then what would you suggest I order?"

"A firing squad for that imbecile cook. I'm sure he would even burn boiling water," he said, pushing his plate away in disgust.

The waitress arrived, saving me from another of Silas' long diatribes. I looked over at the pontificating nemesis of chefs worldwide and played it safe by ordering a Mount Washington organic beer.

I looked out the window at the Presidentials and was greeted by another jaw-dropping twilight. The setting sun in the west was illuminating the peaks of the mountains, making it look like they were on fire. The pink and orange colors contrasted against the dark ridge line shadows. This truly was God's country.

"Hey, gorgeous," Emily said as she arrived and sat down.

"You're late," I observed, "but at least you showed up this time."

"*Why you gotta be sooo mean?*" Emily sang out, channeling Top 40 radio.

"Funny, but I always hear a femme fatale song when you walk in a room."

"*Touché héros de guerre,*" Emily said in a sexy French voice.

My organic draft arrived signaling a détente to the insults. I swigged down a few swallows of my hoppy ale and wondered why Emily was so anxious to have dinner with me. I didn't have to wait long for an answer.

"So I've been thinking about your riddles," Emily began after sampling her Moscow Mule. "How is it you came across the first riddle anyway?"

"It was hidden inside of the cicada."

"What???" Emily nearly choked on her drink. "Are you performing autopsies on insects now?"

"Hardly," I replied. "I was sitting with Father Callaghan the other night. He was drunk, boiled as an owl, and he started rambling on about my family and how someone had broken into the Rectory looking for something valuable. When I asked him what he thought the thieves were looking for, he pulled out the cicada. I didn't take him seriously at first so he chopped the bug's head with his whiskey glass and then started mixing his metaphors. The last thing he said to me before staggering out the door was to study the cicada. I didn't notice the rolled-up piece of paper inside the exoskeleton until the next morning. When I heard that Callaghan was murdered in cold blood I went to the chapel. Quinn was there. We found another copy of the riddle hidden in the walls."

"That's quite a story. You think Father Callaghan was killed for the bug?"

"I have no idea, but I plan to find out."

"And how do you intend to do that?" she asked.

"By solving the riddles and seeing where they lead me."

"You mean *us*. I really want to tag along, Darby. We'd make a great team. I've got a lot of resources at my disposal."

"The problem is I don't know where to start," I admitted.

"Well I do," Silas butted in from his nearby table.

"Have you been eavesdropping on us this whole time?" I asked.

"When one hears the word 'cicada', one can't help but take notice. Did you know the cicada is a symbol of resurrection and immortality? Aristotle was even said to be enamored with the pest. He ate dozens every day. Maybe the chef should put them on the menu. Can't be any worse than the slop he's serving now—"

"Did you say you figured out where we need to go?" I asked, interrupting his bug cuisine lecture.

"Yes and no. I know of another who can help us, but we must leave Bretton Woods posthaste," Silas said.

"Why the hell didn't you tell me this earlier?" I demanded.

"One can't travel on an empty stomach. Just ask Marco Polo. He found out the hard way when—"

"Please! Not another story," I begged.

"Now, Silas, exactly how are we leaving Bretton Woods? None of us has a car," Emily pointed out.

"I have the finest chariot available, my lady, and more importantly it's French."

***

The walk to the parking lot with Silas in tow was a thousand times more painful than taking a stroll with the Marquis de Sade

96

himself. I was starting to believe that Silas was actually the reincarnation of the French aristocrat minus the libertine sexuality, but as soon as he started talking about that damn car, the perverse eroticism that had been absent finally made an appearance.

Opening the storage shed, Silas took hold of the waterproof car cover and quickly removed it like a magician yanking the linen off a fine china-laden table. I took a step back to better observed the machine in front of me.

"This is your car?" I asked, both bewildered and jealous.

"*Mais oui*," he answered in a horrendous French accent, "but it really was Brigitte's baby. She loved this car and drove it everywhere."

"Who's Brigitte?" I asked as I began to walk around the car, tracing its fine curves with my open hand.

"Who's Brigitte?! For god's sakes man, have you no culture at all? She's only the most seductive siren ever to grace the silver screen. Ah, I remember it like yesterday. It was July and the wildflowers were erupting in color all over Paris. *L'amour est dans l'air.* Love was in the air!" he yelled." BB—that was my pet name for her—and I were working on the movie set of *Le Trou Normand.* I must say that she was quite a looker and we were crazy for love," Silas purred as he winked at me and jabbed me in the ribs with one of his elbows.

I stood there with a blank look on my face, but Emily as usual put the pieces together quickly.

"Wait a minute, you're not talking about—"

"That's exactly who I'm talking about," Silas said, "but I prefer to call her my third ex-wife. She had a weakness for powerful and good-looking men like myself. She wasn't able to control herself around me. I bought her the Peugeot as a wedding gift."

I mentally began to do the math in my head, trying to figure out if it was even possible that Silas could have been married to that French bombshell. She would have been around eighteen and Silas…how the hell old was he? I blinked my eyes, returning to the present as Silas' voice continued to drone on.

"This fine automobile is a '58 rear wheel drive, convertible Peugeot 403 Sept in a one-of-a-kind Shell Pink custom color. It has a diesel engine and a manual four-speed transmission that produces sixty-five breakneck horsepower. Its greatest feature, if you ask me, has to be the front seats which fold down and lay flat with the back seat cushions forming a couchette, that means a double bed for all you non-French speakers among us," he said, looking at me.

I gazed at the white-walled tires, trying to not listen. The car appeared to be in immaculate condition, ageless like Silas himself.

"When's the last time you drove this?" I asked, interrupting Silas' graphic demonstration of the amorous backseat.

"Let's see…I believe it was in '81. Jacques Cousteau was in town and together we were raising quite a ruckus when we ran out of crab dip—"

Ugh. I didn't want to hear another long-winded, pointless story. "Sorry to interrupt, but where exactly are we going in this fine automobile? Can you show me on a map?" I asked.

"Well, it appears that we're looking for a proverbial white whale, therefore I think it is most apropos to say, that the 'place we are seeking is not down in any map; true places never are.'

Where we are going, my friends, there are no maps, just legends, landmarks, and poppycock."

"Sounds wonderful," I mumbled to Emily. She hushed me and slapped me on the arm.

"If it exists at all, it will be a venerable Shangri-La," Silas continued. "Speaking of Shangri-La, did you know that the French originally included a copy of the Kama Sutra with this car? Brigitte and I did a lot of reading on that couchette."

I thought I might actually throw up.

"Silas, what ever happened with you and BB? Why didn't it work out?" Emily asked.

"That's a long story," Silas said wistfully.

"Aren't all your stories long?" I blurted out. Emily shot me the stink eye, forcing me to apologize. "I'm sorry, Silas, that was rude of me. Please continue. I would like to know about you and BB, that is if it isn't too painful a memory for you."

"Well as you know, I don't like to talk too much about myself—" he began again as I rolled my eyeballs and bit my tongue, "—but BB…she began to care more about animals than people. It was always animal rights this and animal rights that. She talked nonstop about these beasts of burden until I couldn't take it anymore. I was trying to think of a way to cut it off nice and easy with her and then a bright idea came to me as I was shopping for the holidays. I stopped into one of the finest furriers in all of New York City and I purchased her the most regal Russian sable fur coat I could find. Needless to say, she left me faster than a New York minute. My friend Johnny used to say that a 'New York minute was the time interval between a Manhattan traffic light turning green and the guy behind you honking his horn.' BB was so pissed about the coat, she just ran the red light before I could even honk my horn. She never did return to me. I hear she started her own animal rights foundation and is still pissing people off all these years later. That's my BB, following her heart."

"So what happened to the coat?" I asked.

"Oh, she kept the coat in spite of her feelings about animals. I heard she gave it to some young boy from Alabama years later. Joe Broadway or something like that."

Emily and I just stared at each other for a moment, not knowing what to believe.

"Well that's enough chit-chatting about the past. We have a long evening drive in front of us, so climb aboard you two. And don't you dare get any ideas about that couchette."

Silas started the diesel engine. The roar was deafening. I thought the entire RAF was preparing for takeoff as the engine revved and then idled. Stealth would not be a factor tonight. A marching band would hear us coming a mile away. Emily and I climbed into the backseat.

"All set!" I yelled to Silas.

"What?" he yelled back.

I banged on the side of the car and motioned with my hand indicating that we were ready to go. Silas gunned the engine and we sped away at the breakneck speed of thirty-five miles per hour. The smell of diesel fumes drifted in through the windows. We'd be lucky not to die of asphyxiation before we reached our destination. Emily just laughed and smiled at me. I smiled back at her, feeling like I was nineteen again.

"Don't get any ideas, sailor," she said with a grin.

CHAPTER 11

Finnegan Doyle rested against an old growth tree admiring the multicolored hues of the North Country foliage. Autumn had descended on the Presidential Range awakening the blazing red maples, golden domed aspens, and magnificent copper oaks. The patchwork of color grew in massive colonies that blanketed the granite outcrops of the White Mountains. Finnegan thought about the first time he saw Pando, an ancient colony of quaking aspen trees in Utah encompassing over a hundred acres. Pando had more than forty thousand above-ground stems with an average age of 130 years old. The deep fireproof root system had existed for over eighty thousand years, making it one of the oldest known living systems in the world.

Surveying Aqua-Nord's ongoing deforestation efforts in the distance, Finnegan's blood screamed out for vengeance. Man's ignorance and continuing belief that the Earth's resources were infinite and destined to be consumed would be humanity's ultimate downfall. Finnegan might not be able to save the world, but he sure as hell would protect the Great North Woods up to his dying breath. Given the chance, he'd take Pickford Marsh and all of Aqua-Nord to hell with him.

The sudden sound of engines nearby caused Finn to duck back into the safety of the thick forest. Positioning himself between two large glacial boulders on top of a thirty-foot high cliff, Finnegan flattened himself and waited along the side of the roughly hewed trail below him. He was surprised to find visitors this far out and off the marked hiking trails. Maybe they were lost or maybe they were looking for him. Either way, he would blend into the forest and wait for them to move on.

The four-wheelers stopped just below the cliffs from him. Rifle cases and duffle bags were strapped to the side and rear of the vehicles. *Hunters perhaps,* he thought to himself. The taller of the two riders dismounted his ATV and inspected the woods around him. Dusk was beginning to set in and it was unusual for hunters to be out this far in the wilderness at this time of day. If they turned around now, they would have to finish their trek back to the main road in complete darkness.

Satisfied with what he saw or didn't see, the taller of the two men signaled to his companion to join him at the base of the cliffs. Their voices were muffled, but they seemed to be discussing something of importance. They pulled out a map and then pointed down slope. After a minute of additional conversation, they shouldered two mammoth duffle bags along with their rifles and set off downhill, leaving their vehicles behind. *Where in the world are you two going?*

Finn decided against trying to follow them. Instead he'd settle in and wait for them to return. It was no use trying to track them in the dark and he wasn't about to risk exposing his position by making noise. Reconnaissance would be far easier from his perch atop the cliffs. He could always reconnoiter the area down slope later in the daylight and figure out the intent of the two trespassers to his world.

***

I had no idea where we were going, nor did I really care. I was just happy to get out from under the microscope of Bretton Woods for a little while. Although we had a chaperone, it felt good to be alone with Emily. The rumbling diesel engine and Silas' incessant but muffled talking afforded us some element of privacy in the backseat of the Peugeot.

We gazed at each other quietly for the first few miles as the memories circulated inside each of our heads, causing random smiles and laughs. Emily finally broke the silence when she asked, "Why did you leave me?"

Damn, she couldn't have started with something easier? The smile disappeared from my face as I pondered how to answer.

"I was nineteen, Emily. I had to find my own way in the world."

"I know, but you could have come back. You just gave up on me. You gave up on us. You never gave us a chance."

"I didn't give up on you, I just didn't want to live a predetermined life. If I had stayed or if I had come back, I would have drowned, overburdened by my family's expectations."

"You wouldn't have drowned. I would have been there to help you stay afloat," she said as tears started to fill her eyes.

"That wouldn't have been fair to you," I said, lowering my own eyes. "I couldn't put you through that."

"That wasn't your choice to make. It was mine, you idiot," she said, punching me in the shoulder.

"I can see that now, but at nineteen I thought I knew it all."

"Well, you don't know anything. Do you know how many nights I waited at home, hoping you would call? Do you know how many bad relationships I let myself get trapped in because I wanted to feel loved? I allowed guys to walk all over me because I didn't want them to leave me. You really screwed me up, Darby, and I stayed that way for a long time."

"I'm sorry," I said honestly. "I did what I thought was right."

"Sorry doesn't cut it," she said. "We all have problems, but normal people work their way through them. They don't run away from them and never look back. That's what cowards do, not Medal of Honor winners."

"I've spent every day of my life trying to find meaning and purpose. Do you know what it's like to go through each day not trusting a single person?"

"You could have trusted me," she whispered.

"I loved you at one time, Emily," I confessed, "but I never really trusted you."

"Why?" she demanded between quiet sobs. "Why couldn't you trust me?"

"Because I knew you really loved someone else."

Emily couldn't hide the surprise and fear on her face. I could tell she was questioning how much I knew and she was unsure of what to say. She looked at me for a long time and then turned her head and stared out the window, into the darkness of the night. We passed back through the Notches on our way into the unknown.

One thing was certain: if Emily and I were to ever have a future, we would first have to reconcile our past.

***

The roar of the ATVs' engines coming to life jolted Finn awake. The sky was just starting to lighten in the east as the two trespassers maneuvered their vehicles around and headed back in the direction in which they had come the night before.

Checking his watch, Finn calculated that the two men had been gone almost twelve hours. They had to have camped somewhere in the woods overnight. Oddly, their duffle bags were nowhere to be seen. The bags were missing and had not been reattached to the four-wheelers. This pissed Finn off to no end. Hadn't they heard of the hikers' credo of 'pack it in, pack it out'?

Fifteen minutes after the sound of the engines had faded, Finn rose from his hiding spot and stretched. His body ached from an uncomfortable sleep. He chastised himself for drifting off in the middle of the night. They could have crept up behind him. He felt ashamed. His father had taught him better than that.

Looking further down slope, Finn smiled at the sight. He was pleased that the lower woods were encased in an early morning fog. The low-lying cloud would mask his inspection of the area and dampen any sound he might make. They couldn't have travelled too far with their overloaded duffle bags due to the lack of light. The steepness of the terrain also would have made the bags difficult for them to balance on their shoulders.

Whatever they were carrying it was sure to be a pain in the ass. *Let's see what we can find,* Finn thought to himself as he repelled down the cliff face and entered the fog.

Finn hadn't travelled more than a hundred yards down slope when he encountered his first clue. Lying in the leaf litter beside an old growth evergreen was a soggy pack of cigarettes. The robin's egg-blue pack was easy enough to spot amongst the brown pine needles and cones. He desperately wanted a smoke but decided against it as the smell would be detectable over a considerable distance and he couldn't afford to reveal his location to anyone who might be nearby. Inserting the pack of smokes into his rucksack, Finn continued downhill and headed east towards Crawford Notch.

Finn thought it was odd that the two men and their ATVs had shown up from the south. There was no civilization south of here, only the deep boreal forest and hard living. It puzzled him even more that when they left, they headed back in that direction. Back to the south, back to nowhere.

After traveling another forty yards, Finn stopped, unable to go any further. He peered over a sheer cliff face that disappeared into the fog below. What the hell? They couldn't have gone over the cliff last night in the dark. Where did they go then? Finn turned in a complete circle trying to spot anything that might give him a clue. Nothing. No campsite, no additional trash. It was like they were never here. He doubled back, slowly retracing his footsteps. He must have missed something on his way down. Pausing at the spot where he originally found the cigarettes, Finn looked down and noticed a small, flat oval-shaped object lying on the ground. Picking it up and turning it over in his hand, Finn realized what he was looking at. He dropped it as quickly as he could before bending over and vomiting on the bloody human ear below him.

Oh dear God, what did they do?

Regaining his composure, Finn raced up the hill back to his cliff-top perch. He looked south into the deepest part of the old growth forest and wondered what monsters lurked out there. He was determined to find out as he headed into the unknown, following the ATV tracks into the black forest.

The tracks had come within a half-mile of the AMC hut where his guest was sheltered, which surprised Finn. Common sense said to stay away from people and any unwelcome eyes, but the two goons ignored the risk. Their arrogance was sickening to Finn. They traversed the area around Thoreau Falls before plunging further south into the wilds of the White Mountains. Their course made no sense. There was nothing out there. Finn hiked another two miles over rough terrain before deciding to turn back toward the Zealand Falls hut. He was ill-prepared to camp, which he would have to do if he travelled much further, and he didn't want to get stuck out here after nightfall. He needed to check in on his guest anyway, but his curiosity was indeed piqued. *I'll see you two again*, he thought.

***

The deceleration of the car followed by the rhythmic clicking of the turn signal woke me from an uncomfortable sleep. Sometime during the night I had nodded off, planting my face into the side window of the car. Opening my eyes, I recognized the gray stone balls mounted on pedestals that graced the edges of the Ledyard Bridge. As we crossed the fog-encased Connecticut River, a group of early morning rowers disappeared into the mist below us. The Peugeot labored as it climbed the steep hill of the opposite shore until we saw the expansive Green of Dartmouth spread out before us.

Silas pulled into the porte-cochere of the Hanover Inn on the southern edge of the Green and cut his deafening Spitfire engine.

"…and that's how Ernie Hemmingway and I ended up fighting the entire French Foreign Legion," Silas said, concluding what must have been a marathon story that lasted throughout the night.

"How…interesting," Emily answered in her most polite voice even though neither one of us heard a single word Silas had said since the diesel engine first roared to life.

"What are we doing at Dartmouth?" I asked, wiping the sleep out of my eyes and wondering how an hour and half trip could take us three times as long.

"Visiting old friends," Silas drawled.

"What old friends?" I replied, becoming frustrated with his blasted doublespeak.

"Why, a ship's captain, a poet, and a glorious old bulldog of course. They hold the answers you seek and the directions we need. Come now, we mustn't be late. The gatekeeper can be quite incorrigible if he's kept waiting."

Silas led us across the street and onto a diagonal path that dissected the open Green. Dartmouth was a special place to both Emily and me, a place marker from our past. The point where our two lives first crossed. I looked at Emily, remembering the first time I saw her sitting on the Green. Her hair pulled back into a dark ponytail and her deep blue eyes reflecting the last rays of a late autumn sunset. Sensing my gaze, Emily turned her head and smiled at me. She reached over and held my hand ever so gently in hers as we walked toward the north end of the Green. Emily must have felt the emotion as well. She had not forgotten the significance of this place.

Sometimes the pull of a memory is even stronger than the repelling force of a broken heart. Emily's touch ignited my skin. I knew I could easily love her again, if I could only learn to love myself first.

"Look around and tell me, my two cherubs, what do you see?" asked Silas.

"I see the Rollins Chapel," Emily offered.

I leaned over and whispered in her ear. "I only see the past."

"I see a building within a building, a temple within a body, and an old facade hiding the new. Our answers await," Silas said, pointing to bricked-faced exterior of the Rauner Library. We passed the four granite columns standing sentry and entered the Temple of Knowledge.

The Rauner Special Collections Library at Dartmouth College is a magnificent structure. From the outside it looks like a typical Ivy League building: regal and stately with red bricks accented by bands of white granite and an ornate roof trim. A trio of enormous floor-to-ceiling windows flanked each side of the building, allowing a cascade of natural light to flow in and bathe the interior in a warm glow. Four soaring Greek columns guarded the entrance. Once you cross the threshold and enter the interior, you are greeted by an entirely new structure – a lantern-like vault. This building within a building is staggering and not easy to access the treasures hidden within.

"State your name and reason for wanting access to the special collections," a decrepit male research librarian commanded.

"For god's sake, Horatio, you know who I am," Silas squawked back.

"The rules are the rules, Silas, and since I know you to be a logger-headed, fen-sucked canker-blossom, I need to know the nature of your visit."

"Well, you as a gore bellied, rump-fed codpiece should already know the nature of my business," Silas huffed, casting a steely eye on the gatekeeper of the special collections.

"Oh this is going to be good," I whispered to Emily as we gazed with open mouths at the two magniloquent centenarians who lobbed insults at each other. The aged librarian leaned over his massive oak desk and glared at Silas who still had his hackles up.

"Your Shakespearean insults are indeed improving, but you are still a monstrously non-intuitive lackey and a debased buttock-rimming delinquent who has delusions of adequacy!"

Silas' face had turned blood red as he repositioned himself so that he was nose-to-nose with the offending librarian. "And you are a dreadfully pedestrian dolt and a revolting heart-sickening obfuscation of all that is good!"

They continued hurling insults at each other for another full minute before a smile broke out on the librarian's face. "Silas, you really need to visit more often. I miss this type of cock-crowing with you."

"Indeed," Silas replied, wiping the sweat from his brow. "Darby S. Weeks and Ms. Emily Baines, may I introduce you to Horatio Bollerud, my older but obviously less handsome brother."

"Charmed to meet you, Ms. Baines," Horatio said, grabbing Emily's hand and drawing it to his lips. Emily giggled at the gesture.

"Careful, Horatio, I believe she is already spoken for," Silas stated while winking at me.

"We're not a couple," I informed Horatio as Emily stuck her tongue out at me.

"Indubitably," he answered back.

"Enough of this chin-wag," Silas said, cutting off the pleasantries. "We've come seeking your help, Horatio. We need access to some of the rare books in your collection."

"Which books do you seek?" Horatio responded.

"We would prefer to just browse the stacks," I said, not really knowing how much I should trust Horatio and having no idea what we were looking for in the first place, anyway.

"You'd prefer to just browse the stacks?" Horatio repeated back to me. "Would you also like someone to massage your feet or perhaps a hot toddy to quench your thirst from your lengthy journey?" he asked. "Nobody is allowed to just browse the stacks."

I looked at Silas hoping for some assistance, but he was preoccupied with a large wooden globe.

"How do we view the books then?" Emily asked in her sweetest voice.

"Let me review the rules for you," Horatio said with a sigh. "There are no backpacks, computer cases, handbags, coats, hats, pens, food, or drinks allowed in the reading rooms. A photo ID is required of all users. You must request materials from me. I will retrieve the requested items and will hold your identification while you use the materials. You may not mark or alter the materials in any way. No special collections materials may leave the reading rooms without permission from the College Archivist or me. Any questions?"

111

"Yes. When did you become such a blowhard, Horatio?" Silas yelled without lifting his eyes from the globe.

"These rules exist for the materials' protection. There are no exceptions," Horatio said, walking toward Silas who was now spinning the globe recklessly. "Stop that!" he yelled, placing his hand on the sphere.

I decided to trust him. "Horatio, if we can't browse the materials then we will require some additional assistance to refine our search," I said.

He smiled. "How can I be of help?"

"We have a riddle that we are trying to solve. Perhaps you can make some sense out of it?"

"Riddles?" he said with a twinkle in his eye. "Let's hear it."

I cleared my throat while removing the folded paper from my pocket. I looked at Silas and Emily, hoping I was doing the right thing by trusting Horatio.

With a drizzly November in my soul,
Behind a Michael Smalle penned letter is foretold,
The heir to the king of coal marks the view in which you seek
In Concord, the silhouette and bones, the perfect gleek.

"Hmm, a conundrum indeed," Horatio said, stroking his chin. He paced back and forth repeating the riddle under his breath. "Can I see the paper?"

Hoping he could decipher its meaning, I handed it to him. Horatio read the riddle aloud off the paper while he continued to pace.

"We think the king of coal might be a reference to Joseph Stickney," I said, hoping that it might help Horatio.

112

"Got it!" Horatio yelled out, startling us.

"Darn it!" Silas bellowed back. "It's impossible that you solved it that quickly."

"All it required was a brain bigger than a dingle berry, dear brother."

"You know what the riddle means?" I asked.

"Well, the first line is an obvious reference to *Moby Dick*," he said matter-of-factly, "and Silas was correct to lead you to me because there are only a select few who would understand the significance of the second line."

"What does it mean?" Emily asked excitedly.

He started toward the lantern-like vault. "Come with me."

"I thought browsing the stacks was not allowed," I said as we entered the rare book vault.

"There's no need to browse the stacks, Mr. Weeks, if you know what you are looking for. Do either of you two know what is kept here in the special collections?"

Emily and I shrugged our shoulders. "We're both Dartmouth alums, but I've never been in here," I admitted.

"We have one of the largest Robert Burn collections in the world totaling over two thousand items. We also have extensive works by Erskine Caldwell, Joseph Conrad, Charles Dickens, T.S. Elliot, William Faulkner, and Robert Frost," he said with pride. "As well as works by Jack London, Ernest Hemmingway, Shakespeare, George Santayana, Rudyard Kipling, Henry James, Aldous Huxley, and one of the finest Don Quixote collections in the world."

"And don't you dare forget our friend Winnie's letters and books," Silas added as he pulled a bound novel from the shelf.

I read the name of Sir Winston Churchill on the spine. "You knew Churchill?"

"Indeed," the two men said in unison.

"I was one of Winnie's closest confidants and his chief speech writer during the war," Silas announced. "We put away drams of Scotch, chased women, and cursed the Nazis until we were hoarse."

I rolled my eyes, not believing for a minute that Silas knew Churchill. Then he cleared his throat and started bellowing out one of Churchill's finest oratorical moments from memory.

Silas's deep voice echoed through the voluminous book chamber as he recounted all the places that the British would stand and fight against the Nazis. Whether conflict came from the skies, seas, fields, or on the beaches of their island nation, the British would put up a ferocious fight and never give up. I thought Churchill himself was speaking through Silas at that very moment. It unexpectedly moved me.

"Your finest hour, dear brother," Horatio whispered. He wiped a tear from his eye and blew his nose into a handkerchief.

"Indeed," Silas responded. "I do miss that old dipsomaniac."

"Silas, do you recall that splendid night when Winnie convinced the entire Rockettes dance troop to join us in recreating the D-day landings? We commandeered that cog railroad car and stormed the summit right after their summer review show at the hotel."

"How can I ever forget? That's where I met my second ex-wife," Silas said longingly.

"How did all these rare books end up here?" I asked, interrupting their walk down memory lane while I pulled out a bound Ambrose Bierce book.

"Dartmouth is a very old institution, Mr. Weeks," Horatio replied. "The list of alumni and former professors are quite distinguished. Pictures of many of these Dartmouth greats are hung throughout the college. Many of these alumni donate their books and rare collections to us after they die. For example, the core of the Ambrose Bierce collection that you are leafing through now was donated by George Matthew Adams in 1947."

"Ambrose once wrote that 'love is a temporary insanity curable only by marriage'," Silas said with a smirk. "I wish I had learned that a lot earlier."

"Ambrose also mysteriously disappeared in war-torn Mexico around 1913. He is a national treasure that most people don't even know about," Horatio said while shaking his head. "These books and special collections are an invaluable treasure full of mystery and intrigue. That's why they are so well guarded by me."

"With all due respect, Horatio, can we get back to our mystery?" I said, aware of how much time we were wasting.

"Ah yes, the riddle. As I mentioned, the first line of the enigma is a direct quote from the first pages of *Moby Dick*, but it is the second line of your riddle that is so intriguing to me."

"*Behind a Michael Smalle penned letter…*" Silas scratched his head. "I can't recall anyone famous named Michael Smalle," he said.

"That's because there is no one named Michael Smalle. The extra 'e' on the end of 'Smalle' is a dead giveaway that it's really an anagram," Horatio announced while grabbing another leather-bound book from the stack.

"An anagram for what?" Emily inquired.

"Call me Ishmael," I said, surprising myself and everyone else.

"Indeed," Horatio answered with one eyebrow raised.

"Did Ishmael write a letter in the story?" Emily asked, likely feeling embarrassed that she had never read the famous book.

Silas beat his brother to the answer. "No, Ishmael is the narrator and lone survivor of the ill-fated whaling voyage."

"Then what letter is the riddle referring to?" Emily asked, clearly becoming frustrated.

"I believe the riddle references a letter written by Herman Melville himself in 1853."

"Oh pish posh, brother. How in the world would you know that?" Silas asked.

"Because the letter is right here," he said, holding up a first edition of *Moby Dick*.

"Inconceivable," Silas roared.

"There are over 230 first editions of *Moby Dick* in our prestigious collection printed in over thirty different languages, but only one first edition has a letter written in Melville's own hand bound inside it." Horatio held the book above his head. "I give you the Pittsfield letter dated December 14, 1853," he said, opening the book and placing it on a reading table for all of us to see.

We looked at the letter in silence for a long moment before I verbalized what we were all thinking. "It's a bunch of chicken scratch that I can't even read."

"It's called penmanship, Mr. Weeks," Silas trilled. "Something that has been lost on the youth of today."

"What does it say?" Emily asked.

Horatio pulled a silver-chained monocle from his breast pocket and began examining the text in detail. After a minute he reported, "It appears this letter is nothing more than a social correspondence between Melville and a woman referred to as 'My Lady Countess'. He's discussing his availability to attend her Christmas or Christmas Eve dinner parties with three other women."

"That sly old fox," Silas said with a grin.

Emily looked disappointed. "How's that supposed to help us?"

"Look on the back of the letter...in the corners," I said in a daze, knowing what would be found there.

Horatio turned the page and laid the book down on the reading table allowing us all to see the backside of the letter. It was faded and yellowed with age, but there were two distinct markings in opposite corners. In one corner was the letter 'A' written in red ink and in the second corner was what appeared to be a flattened or a misshapen 'W'.

"The mystery deepens," Horatio said, gazing at me with renewed interest.

"Darby, how did you know there would be markings on the back in the corners?" Emily asked with a confused looked on her face.

I looked at all three of them, knowing that they were waiting for a logical explanation from me. The memories continued to return to me like burns from a cigarette. Short and violent bursts of pain followed by visible scars that cut into my flesh. How does one admit to something they have spent their whole life denying and running from? In an instant, I knew my days of running were over. Poised at the edge a cliff with nowhere to go, I decided to finally admit the truth to myself and to them.

"I wrote the marks myself a long, long time ago."

CHAPTER 12

Cold water dripped down my face as I looked into the library's bathroom mirror wondering who was gazing back at me. I didn't know anymore. I'd been insulated from my past all these years. The Navy didn't care who I was before I walked through 'freedom's front door' and enlisted. "Just do your job and you'll be all right," the recruiting petty officer had told me. I followed orders and blended in, disappearing into the machine. I managed to successfully recreate myself, forgetting all that came before, at least until that damn medal was draped over my head like an executioner's noose. The time had come to place my cards on the table and settle up.

The imaginary voices of the literary giants fell silent as I reentered the reading room. Silas and Horatio sat alone at one of the tables, examining the marks on the letter. Emily was nowhere to be found. The brothers watched me with suspicious eyes as I approached them and sat down at the table. I cleared my throat and waited for the Inquisition to commence.

"Shall we wait for Emily?" I said after a tense minute had passed in silence.

"No," Horatio answered, "she said she needed to check in with New York."

"There's something we need to discuss with you in private anyway," Silas added. "You say you made the marks on the Pittsfield letter a long time ago?"

"Yes, as a child under the direction of my father."

"How old were you?" Horatio asked without emotion.

"Six…maybe seven years old."

"Did you know that the original gift of the Melville collection from George Matthew Adams, the one that contained this fine first edition of Moby Dick, used to contain two bound letters within: the Pittsfield letter and another?"

I swallowed hard before answering. "Yes, I'm aware that there were two letters."

"The second letter was egregiously stolen out of the archive in 1976. Do you know anything about that?" Horatio asked.

"Yes, my father took it from the archive." I remembered that cold November day. "He had me copy it in my best penmanship. After I had finished the task, I placed it in a jar and threw it into the ocean," I said, wiping away a tear that had begun to streak down my face.

"Do you know who Melville's second letter was addressed to?" Silas asked.

"Nathaniel Hawthorne," I said in a trace-like voice.

"Nathaniel Hawthorne?" Horatio repeated. "Jeezum Crow, Darby. The 'A' must be a scarlet letter!" He jumped out of his seat and rushed into the stacks, returning a few moments later holding Hawthorne's magnum opus.

"How is *The Scarlet Letter* going to aid us in solving this intolerable quandary?" Silas asked.

"We should review the riddle," I said, becoming lucid again.

"It appears we have successfully deciphered the first two lines," Horatio said. "Let's turn our attention to the next two."

The heir to the king of coal marks the view in which you seek
In Concord, the silhouette and bones, the perfect gleek.

"As I mentioned before, I think the king of coal is a reference to Joseph Stickney," I said.

"And we have just learned that you, Darby, have made the marks in the text…"
The two brothers looked at me, waiting for me to confess.

"Yes, I am the heir," I said, realizing the jig was up, "but I still don't believe I'm truly related to Joseph Stickney. My understanding is that he never had any children with Princess Carolyn."

"One need not be related to be an heir to a fortune," Silas said. "I do recall that my dear acquaintance Mindy Rose left twelve million dollars to her pooch named Woe."

"That's right, brother. I haven't thought about Mindy in years. She was one hell of a pivot blocker on the roller derby circuit. She skated under that pseudonym…um, what was it again, Silas?"

"Vulva Display of Power," he said resolutely.

"Yes, that's it!" Horatio said excitedly. "She had some epic battles in Madison Square Garden against her arch enemy—"

"Clitty Clitty Bang Bang," Silas blurted out, finishing his brother's sentence.

"Indeed."

"How in the world does a roller derby skater earn enough to leave millions to her dog?" I asked, thinking I was having my leg pulled again by the Bollerud brothers.

"Mindy got into real estate after her skating days were over. She changed her name several times in an effort to find happiness and success. She ended up marrying a multi-millionaire," Silas added.

"You've got to be kidding me. Vulva Display of Power was really—?"

"Yep, one in the same," Silas confirmed.

"Truth is many times stranger than fiction, my dear boy," Horatio declared. "I have no doubt that you are related to and the rightful heir of the Stickney fortune."

I let Horatio's words sink in as I considered the implications.

"I suggest we keep any further revelations to ourselves," Horatio added. "The last thing we need is the CEO of Tither Publishing discovering private information."

I looked at Horatio with a puzzled look on my face.

"Your…ahem…girlfriend, Darby, is the new Queen of Mean."

"She's not my girlfriend."

Silas and Horatio nodded their heads disbelievingly. I pondered the idea of Emily using me to gain information that she could later leverage to blackmail others or me. Was Emily really capable of that?

"Let's think about the next line in riddle," Silas said. "In Concord, the silhouette and bones, the perfect gleek."

"What does gleek mean?" I asked. "I've never heard of that word before."

"Gleek has a couple of meanings," Horatio answered. "Shakespeare used it in his plays. It can mean a three-person game of cards or—"

"A trick or deception," Silas said, finishing the sentence.

"Deception seems to be a better fit in our riddle," I observed.

"Agreed, and I believe the mention of bones might reference a grave," Horatio said.

"Whose grave?" I asked.

Silas held the parchment up to his eyes and reread it slowly while mouthing the words. "Well, if we take everything into consideration, I do believe this line indicates that we need to visit a cemetery."

"Whose grave?" I repeated.

"I believe the scarlet letter—the red 'A' that you wrote on the back of the Pittsfield letter as a child—is the clue to solving this part of the riddle," Horatio declared. "If your little red 'A' truly alludes to Hawthorne's greatest work, then perhaps the author's final resting place is where you should look next?"

"Where's Hawthorne buried?" I asked.

"Concord, Massachusetts," they both answered in unison.

"Then we leave for Concord immediately," I said.

"That's not such a good idea," Horatio indicated while pointing towards one of the windows out on the mezzanine level.

Sleet and freezing rain had starting pelting the street and walkways outside of Webster Hall.

"I agree," Silas said. "The weather looks treacherous. I've already taken the liberty of booking us rooms at the Hanover Inn. We shall stay the night and commence our journey in the morning."

"Fine with me. I could use a good night's sleep," I said cracking my neck.

"Good luck with that, old boy. They only had two rooms available at the inn," Silas said with a twinkle in his eye.

"Indeed," Horatio added with a laugh.

"In that case, I'll just sleep in the car."

***

Emily excused herself from the reading room at the special collections library while Darby used the restroom. She crossed the street and entered the Rollins Chapel. Built in 1885 as a spiritual center for Dartmouth College, the chapel was spacious and more importantly private. Even though the chapel's grand wooded and arched interior reminded Emily of a capsized ship, she always enjoyed the clerestory and the abundance of light that it let in to the sanctuary.

The building's foldable chairs had been stowed and a temporary labyrinth had been unrolled and laid out on a massive white tarp, covering much of the chapel's now open floor space. Without thinking, Emily began to navigate the maze while her mind wandered. As a 19-year-old Dartmouth undergrad, she imagined someday being married in this very church to the man of her dreams. Unfortunately he had other plans that didn't include her. Emily shook the disillusioned memory out of her head and dialed her office in New York.

"Olivia, I need you to do some digging for me. Find out everything you can about Silas and Horatio Bollerud, then call me back."

Glancing down at her feet, Emily realized she reached one of the labyrinth's many dead ends. She looked up through the massive skylights and frowned at the heavens. Very funny.

***

Finnegan Doyle watched the heavy machinery rip through the glade. It caused his blood to boil in symphonic rage. Mother Earth only had so much skin. Mankind could not continue to strip and peel off the outer layers of the planet without replacing what had been destroyed. He mumbled through clenched teeth a proverb that resonated in the Deep Ecology circles:

> *'When the last tree has been cut,*
> *When the last river has been poisoned,*
> *When the last fish has been caught,*
> *Then we will find out we can't eat money.'*

There will be a heavy price to pay for those foolish enough to commit this ongoing sacrilege, Finn thought to himself.

The sudden silence caused him to press his body flat into the ground and wonder if had he been spotted or his position compromised. He lay immobile, blending into the landscape like a ghost cat. After several minutes, Finn lifted his head, assuring himself that he was still invisible here. He raised his binoculars; what he saw in the clearing before him didn't make sense. The purged ground had been lanced in a coordinated pattern. He watched with interest as workers lowered objects into drilled holes. With swift precision, a man about Finn's age moved from hole to hole checking each placement and making adjustments. Once satisfied that all was as it should be, the man motioned to a team of three who carried out what looked to be a shotgun vertically mounted to a metal platform. The structure was centered in the middle of the clearing. The team covered their ears as the shotgun blast was fired into the ground.

What in the world are you up to, Pickford Marsh?

**

Emily's vibrating cell phone announced the arrival of the call that she had been waiting for all day. She slipped into the empty lounge of the Hanover Inn and answered it like a rabid dog.

"Tell me what I need to know – now."

Olivia was used to her boss's icy demeanor and had already prepared a bulleted version of the information Emily had requested. Olivia read through the list, hearing Emily's heavy breathing on the other end of the phone. As she reached the last item on the list, Olivia paused for dramatic effect before delivering the bombshell.

"Oh my God," Emily replied in disbelief. "Are you sure?"

"I cross-checked it twice myself. There is no doubt. The information is accurate."

"How is that even possible?" Emily asked, not expecting an answer. "Well at least I know who I'm dealing with now. Thanks, I'll be in touch."

"No problem," Olivia said, amazed that her battle-ax of a boss had even said thanks. Maybe her trip home was a good thing after all?

Ending the call, Emily opened the Internet browser on her smartphone and typed in the search words. She spent the next hour reading through each result, becoming more and more intrigued with Silas and Horatio Bollerud's pedigree. *What are you two doing hiding up here and why am I the only person who's bothered to discover your incredible secret?*

CHAPTER 13

Words are like the summer sun: they can do to your heart what a ray of light can do to a fallow field. I read Emily's latest note and felt alive for the first time in ages. My thawing heart matched the Upper Valley's landscape. Winter's early intrusion through the Dartmouth campus had been short-lived as the sun of a new day erased all evidence of the previous night's frozen onslaught. We rose early, eager to find Hawthorne's final resting place and the answers to our riddle.

"I'm not getting back in that vehicle," Emily declared.

"It's all we got," I said, climbing into the backseat of the Peugeot.

"It would be faster to take a stage coach," she continued with a frown on her face.

"Then stay behind and catch the next coach."

Emily looked at me with the eyes of a mass murderer. She had become too accustomed to her Madison Avenue life and wasn't used to people being flippant with her.

"You do know that I've emasculated men for lesser offenses," she said with a fake smile.

I took a swig of my coffee and patted the seat beside me. "There's a full travel mug from the Dirt Cowboy waiting for you, my dear."

Emily evaluated her options and then climbed into the backseat of the car as Silas brought the thundering Peugeot engine back to life. "We'll be lucky if we make it there in three days," she shouted before savoring her java goodness.

"Then we're going to need more coffee," I said, raising my mug in a toast as Silas sped away once again at the breakneck speed of thirty-five miles per hour.

***

Pickford Marsh paced outside his private compound pondering the endless delays that continued to plague what he knew would be his company's crowning jewel. The Granite Pass project would be the first stage of Aqua-Nord's ultimate energy coup. For more than a century, his family's efforts to industrialize the North Country had been thwarted by Joseph Stickney and his blasted progeny. The rival family was nothing more than a miserable pack of hypocrites. Their money came from coal, ripped from the earth. They became born-again stewards of the environment once their millions had already been made. With the recent death of the elder Stickney, Pickford thought the final roadblock had been removed for good. The unexpected return of Darby Stickney Weeks complicated things for him.

129

Their heated meeting was unfortunate. Playing back the scene in his head, Pickford realized that the head-to-head confrontation only encouraged the younger Stickney to stay in Bretton Woods and ask questions which answers needed to stay buried. He doubted the younger Stickney would find anything. Pickford's vibrating cell phone and the voice on the other end changed his mind.

**

The Peugeot's entrance into the Sleepy Hollow cemetery six hours later was enough to wake the long dead and decaying residents. It was billowing smoke and rumbling like a walking artillery barrage. Silas showed tender mercies to Emily and I when he turned off the groaning engine and coasted to a stop.

"…and that's why I told Marlin Perkins to go to H-E double hockey sticks and take his good-for-nothing *Mutual of Omaha Wild Kingdom* show with him. How was I supposed to know the lioness was lactating?"

"Don't even ask," I urged Emily, not wanting to know what story the engine noise shielded us from.

Exiting the car, Silas spread out his arms and said, "What you see before you is one of the oldest cemeteries in the United States and the first to feature a sylvan landscape."

The location could not have been more serene, with woodlands and rolling hills blanketed with pine needles and oak trees. Most well-groomed boneyards left me with a creepy feeling that I couldn't wait to leave behind, but Concord's verdant Sleepy Hollow cemetery was different. It was like a gentle walk through the woods while pondering your existence, at least until Silas opened his mouth again.

"See that retaining wall over there? It was made from recycled stone from the old jail. The very jail where Hank was arrested and held for not paying his taxes," Silas droned.

"Hank who?" Emily asked, encouraging more dribble to fall from Silas' mouth.

"Thoreau," he said, drawing out each syllable like a New England blueblood.

"How much did he owe?" I blurted out, unable to resist joining in on the conversation.

"Two dollars," Silas said.

"He went to jail over two measly dollars?" I asked.

"Hank didn't want his tax dollars going to support war or the continuation of slavery so he refused to pay them; an act of civil disobedience. Thoreau always thought about the common good and actually put his money where his mouth was. I wish more people would follow his example."

"We're losing the light," I observed. "We better hurry up and find Hawthorne."

"We'll find him up there," Silas said with melancholy, pointing to a meandering hill, "along with Hank and Waldo."

A cracked and weathered upright granite tablet marked the path to our destination – *Author's Ridge*. We walked the remaining distance in silence, snaking our way along a path entrenched with tree roots and pine tree waste. Silas halted three quarters of the way up the hill and gestured to a large family marker on the right bearing the name THOREAU chiseled on the bottom.

"Henry Thoreau is actually buried under there?" Emily asked in a hushed tone.

"No, he's under that tiny stone over there," Silas said, pointing two stones away from the family marker.

The plain and diminutive headstone simply read 'HENRY' while a bevy of fountain pens, pencils, and trinkets surrounded the grave.

"Why is all that trash littering his grave?" Emily asked, appalled at the sight.

"It's not trash, my dear," Silas said with a chuckle. "They are tokens left by admirers and soul-mates. Tradition has it that one should leave something behind to mark your visit to Author's Ridge. If it is found acceptable to the patron of your choosing, you'll be rewarded with inspiration, knowledge, or good luck."

As Silas and Emily continued up the hill, I lingered behind looking at Henry Thoreau's modest grave marker. I had read *Walden* as a teenager and identified with Thoreau's decision to leave everything behind and seek a simpler life in the wilderness. I also respected his ability to adhere to the principles to which he preached no matter what the consequences. Stepping off the well-worn path, I knelt down and touched his headstone, brushing a stray pine needle to the ground. I thought about my own father and how there was no physical grave that I could visit. His body was never found. Suicide, they told me, but I knew better. I was there.

The ocean pulsated and festered with raw savagery as wave after wave pummeled the dunes. The gale enhanced high tide chewed at the cliffs beneath Nauset Light. The stout red and white tower offered us a temporary sanctuary from the brutal winds. Sea foam and brine clung to my sweat-soaked body. The wet sand caked to my tiny hands, making the task more difficult. With upmost care I wrote the note in exquisite cursive, keeping vigilant to dot my i's and cross my t's as my father lectured me about the importance of penmanship.

With the task completed, my father handed me a coin emblazoned with a golden double-headed eagle. I placed the note and coin into the Ball Mason jar and sealed it from the elements. My youthful and not yet fully developed brain didn't quite comprehend the task, but I was content to see that it pleased my father. The graying man, seeing the task completed, ushered me and the jar back out into the maelstrom. Leaning into the punishing wind, we inched our way through the beach rose and sea grass until we reached the cliff's edge. Our toes hung over the abyss while sea spray stung our cheeks.   My father looked down at me and smiled, nodding his approval. I cocked my arm, prepared to throw the jar just as my father reached down and grabbed my other hand. He squeezed it tightly not wanting to ever let go. 'Forgive me, my son. Someday I hope you'll understand.' He stepped off the cliff just as I released the jar into the air, spinning and cart wheeling into the darkness below. I watched in horror as they both were swallowed up and cast into a deep black sea. I was only seven.

"Darby, are you coming?" Emily called out from the top of the hill.

"In a minute," I replied in a weak voice.

The late autumn light filtered through the trees. I reached into my coat pocket and left my own token of appreciation on top of Thoreau's diminutive headstone. Silently, I made a wish before standing up and returning to the path. I glanced back, taking one last look at the headless cicada resting peacefully on top of Henry Thoreau. I hoped that my offering and its symbolism would be agreeable to the literary giant. Sprinting up the hill, I caught up to my fellow travel companions. They had stopped at another set of gravestones. A large gray and white upright boulder marked the final resting place of Ralph Waldo Emerson.

It was pretentious, almost vulgar, compared to Thoreau's

humble headstone. The original copper plaque affixed to his grave marker had tarnished over the previous century, leaving an eel green sheen on its face while Emerson's daughter and wife dutifully flanked him.

"Waldo was bigger than life, as his grave reminds visitors today," Silas observed. "He was quite the rock star and showman of his age. I always think of him as a precursor to Liberace – or Lee as I like to call him."

"Did Emerson play piano?" Emily asked.

"No, but in my opinion they shared the same sensibilities," Silas said. "Lee would have liked to be buried like this if he had lived back in the 1800s. Of course, he probably would have demanded that his grave marker be made out of pink quartz with rhinestones."

"Were Emerson, Thoreau, and Hawthorne all friends?" I asked, trying to shake the visual of Liberace's ostentatious grave marker out of my head.

"Waldo was actually a mentor of Thoreau's. He encouraged Hank to keep a journal, but few people – if any – ever cared for Hawthorne," Silas continued. "Good old Waldo outlived them both though. Thoreau died at forty-five and Hawthorne at fifty-nine. Waldo kept sucking wind until he was seventy-eight."

I was growing concerned with the advancing darkness. "Do you have any idea where Hawthorne's grave is?" I asked.

"Oh sure, he's back down the hill just opposite of Hank," Silas replied, pointing back the way we had just come.

"Why did you let us walk all the way up here when Hawthorne was just across the path from Thoreau?"

"It's best to not anger the dead at Author's Ridge," Silas answered. "Waldo would have felt slighted if we had not visited his grave. It was important for you to see the differences in their internments since it mirrors how they lived their lives."

I shook my head, frustrated that Silas had once again found a way to waste our time. We walked in thankful silence back down the hill for another minute. Emily took the lead but stopped just short of Thoreau's grave marker. Catching up to her, I looked down to see what had caught her attention. The flat white marker of Louisa M. Alcott gazed back at me. I waited for the inevitable Silas lecture to commence, but to my surprise he remained stoically mute, not offering any opinion or historical fact. Emily, however, had plenty to say.

"*Little Women* remains one of my all-time favorite books. The sisters passage from childhood to womanhood had a profound effect on me."

"How so?" I asked, wanting to understand more about the part of Emily she rarely let others see.

"It showed me that there was a way to escape the gender constraints forced upon women. That greatness could be achieved despite the best efforts of society, men specifically, to keep 'little women' down," she elaborated.

"Is publishing a scandal rag considered greatness in your eyes?" I asked.

"Nothing could be greater than bringing down the bloated egos of men and exposing their hypocrisy to the world. I offer a sorely needed service to the world."

"Am I to assume then that Jo was your favorite character in *Little Women*?"

"Without a doubt," Emily beamed. "Her strong and willful personality resonated with me."

"Now if I remember the story correctly, didn't the death of her sister Beth cause her to live out the rest of her life with more consideration and kindness for people?" I asked.

Emily gazed at me with a confused look on her face, not knowing how to respond. She chose to end the conversation by just sticking out her tongue at me and punching me in the shoulder.

"The two of you aren't a couple? Yeah right," Silas whispered in my ear while jabbing me in the ribs.

I shot Silas the evilest of looks before he motioned us to the opposite side of the path. Drawing even with Silas, I realized we had found who we were searching for in Concord.

"I never did care for Hawthorne and I'm sure he never would have approved of me either," Silas said. "He was a walking rebuke and a social misfit with a guilty conscience."

I knew his temporary silence was too good to last. Tuning Silas out, I visually took in Hawthorne's final resting spot. It was more substantial than Thoreau's, but less grandiose than Emerson's grave. The Hawthorne family plot was separated from the walking path by a drooping chain. Solitary and limp, it conveyed a certain kind of sadness while three tidy headstones formed a picket, protecting the author's grave like formidable mountains guarding against a barbarian invasion.

"Did you know that one of Hawthorne's relatives was a judge at the notorious Salem witch trials? In an effort to hide his relations to this abomination, Nathaniel added a 'W' to his last name."

"Wait, what did you just say?" I asked as an idea swirled in my brain.

"I said, I never did care for Hawthorne—"

"No, the last bit," I said impatiently.

"He added a 'W' to his name," Silas repeated before adding, "and I'm pretty sure Hawthorne, like Emerson, would feel indignant that he was buried on a repurposed esker. He was no fan of glacial features."

A moment of electrified clarity involving the riddle passed through my body, triggered by Silas' rambling words. I replayed the riddle in my mind.

The heir to the king of coal marks the view in which you seek
In Concord, the silhouette and bones, the perfect gleek.

"When we were up at Dartmouth I thought the second mark on the letter, the one opposite the red 'A', looked like a misshapen or squashed 'W'."

"Yeah, so what?" Emily answered.

"What if that squashed 'W' was really a drawing or a profile of a glacial feature like mountains and valleys?"

Silas paused his ongoing *Lifestyles of the Rich and Famous* dissertation and pondered the idea. "Like a view?"

"Yes, exactly like a view. *The heir to the king of coal marks the view in which you seek,*" I said with excitement. "We're looking for a profile of a mountain valley view."

"But there's no mountains or valleys here," Emily observed.

"The lady is right; Author's Ridge is just a repurposed esker," Silas noted.

"*The king of coal marks the view in which you seek. In Concord, the silhouette and bones, the perfect gleek,*" I repeated. "The king of coal is Joseph Stickney. We're not looking for Hawthorne's grave, we should be looking for Stickney's," I said with excitement. "Silas, where's Joseph Stickney buried?"

He thought for a moment before answering. "Joseph Stickney is buried in the Old North Cemetery…in Concord, New Hampshire."

"We're in the wrong Concord," the three of us said in unison.

***

The barren lane into the Old North Cemetery was rippled with frost heaves and potholes. The Peugeot chewed at the broken pavement, undulating like a lobster boat in a tempest, its diesel engine shattering the silence and grace of an early morning sunrise in the picturesque capital of New Hampshire. Emily and I exited the vehicle, stretched and waited for our tour guide to begin.

"The Old North Cemetery has the distinction of being the oldest burial ground in the capital of the Granite State," Silas said on cue. "Built in 1730, it is the home of Franklin Pierce, the fourteenth President of the United States, as well as the focus of our attention today – Joseph Stickney."

Without intending to, I was becoming quite the connoisseur of bone yards. I noticed an immediate difference between the two Concords' funerary grounds. The look and feel of the cemetery here in New Hampshire was more contrived and a lot less pleasing to the senses. The congestion of headstones made me claustrophobic and uneasy.

"Where do we find the King of Coal?" I asked, wanting to make a quick exit from this city of the dead.

"We'll have to walk a little," Silas said. "Being one of the richest men in the world means being buried with panache."

"What do you think that means?" I asked Emily who was rubbing the early morning cold from her arms.

138

"I'm not sure, but I bet it involves a large phallic symbol," she replied.

We walked amongst the rows of headstones for ten minutes, reading the names of Concord's high society – debutants and politicians from old-wealth families. The grave markers were much more ostentatious than those of the literary greats we had paid our respects to on Author's Ridge, but nothing prepared me for what I saw at Stickney's tomb.

"Oh dear lord. What is that?" I said, pointing just ahead.

"That, my boy, is how the powerful elite ensure they are remembered long after they die," Silas responded.

"Who does he think he is…Pharaoh?" Emily said with disgust.

"More like Zeus if you ask me," Silas quipped.

Rising up out of a spacious well-manicured lawn was Joseph Stickney's tomb – or more accurately his temple. Large and expansive, it looked like something one would find in ancient Greece.

"It looks like a miniature Parthenon," Emily observed.

"At least it isn't phallic," I said.

"He's still overcompensating something," she shot back.

"I think the tomb is understated considering his massive wealth," Silas interjected. "In today's dollars, Stickney would be worth well over nine-hundred million dollars."

"Why would he want to be buried here and not some place more fitting for someone of his stature?" Emily questioned. "Someplace like New York or Athens?"

"Despite what you might imagine about the industrial giants, Ms. Baines, Joseph Stickney loved the outdoors and adored the White Mountains. He wanted to be forever close to the view that inspired him to build his hotel. He was also born in

Concord. Everyone seems to find his or her way back home eventually. Isn't that right, Darby?" Silas said, looking at me.

I was spinning around, taking in the view. "I suppose," I said. There was no obvious mountain silhouette or notched valley that could be seen from Stickney's final resting spot. I started to doubt my theory that the squashed 'W' I had sketched as a child on the back of the second Pittsfield letter was indeed the view we were seeking – a map to the past and a bridge to my future. It had to be here, but there was nothing to be found.

"I don't see any view that resembles the marks on the back of the letter," I said, verbalizing my doubts.

"Sometimes one must look inward to find the treasures that await you out in the world," Silas philosophized while opening the crypt's door and entering the temple of the King of Coal. He stood at the threshold and gestured like a shaman dancing in the wind, motioning us to step further back into the past.

I hesitated, not sure I wanted the knowledge that awaited me inside. Why did I care? Maybe it was best to let my past die along with all its secrets. This wouldn't bring my father or grandfather back and it most certainly would not bring back my friends killed in combat or erase the actions that led to the medal being placed around my neck. I stood frozen, caught in the shallow veil between this world and the ethereal realm of my ancestors, afraid to play the role being offered to me.

"Darby, are you with us?" Emily asked. She was standing next to Silas.

"I don't know why I'm here," I admitted.

"My father's friend Freddy used to say 'to forget one's purpose is the commonest form of stupidity'."

I made eye contact with Emily. Did she remember? She nodded her head as tears welled up in her eyes before she turned away from me. She had said the same thing to me once when we were nineteen. I chose to run back then.

"Time to introduce ourselves to the King of Coal," I announced while stepping through the doorway. My running days were over.

***

The light of the rising sun radiated in from the single window inside the tomb, like a divine message passing between heaven and Earth. There was no shock or verbal chatter among us, just a pure awakening that the knowledge we sought had finally been found. Before us in the tomb was the view, the misshapen 'W', that I had etched on the second Pittsfield letter ages ago. It was so familiar to me yet so unexpected in this chamber of death.

A kaleidoscope of multicolor grandeur from the painted backlit window revealed the view so beloved by Joseph Stickney and so familiar to all of us. We stared at it in silence, as time seemed to stop. I was transported back to a moment in my childhood. I saw the identical image hanging on the wall of our private apartment in the hotel. I heard my father describe all the intricate details of the painting. *Remember it well, my son, for it will lead you to where you need to go.*

Breaking the silence, Emily said what we were all thinking. "It's beautiful."

"Indeed, stunning I'd say. It's like we're actually back in Bretton Woods."

"Is this the view we're searching for, Darby?" Emily asked encroaching on my childhood memory.

"Yes," was all I could manage to say.

Silas began to repeat the final two stanzas of the riddle as we each continued to stare up at the window.

> *Follow the Catamount and Bear oblique*
> *To uncover the past, the truth will reek.*
> *The pit of hell, a well of lost souls*
> *Justice be swift, the names extolled.*

"It seems we have found the view we have been seeking amongst the bones of Joseph Stickney. Now we just need to find the catamount and bear," Silas announced while moving closer to get a better view of the painted window.

"What exactly is a catamount, anyway?"

"Glad you asked, my dear!" Silas beamed.

Oh God, here it comes.

"Catamount happens to be short for 'cat-a-mountain'. The elusive catamount is an Eastern mountain lion that used to live in the upper confines of New England. The clearing of the forests in the 1800s by New Hampshire and Vermont farmers drove the big cats westward since their main food source, the White Tailed Deer, was also eradicated by the falling of the trees. Some claim that the catamount is staging a comeback since its habitat and food source has returned. There are also a lot of reforested nooks and crannies for the reclusive cat to hide within. However, scientists will tell you that there has been no credible sighting of a catamount in New England since 1881."

"Do you think they still exist?" Emily inquired.

"Most certainly, they are here as right as rain. I've personally seen three of these magnificent beasts up in the North Country in the last decade alone."

"Right," I said, "and you lived to tell about it."

"Sometimes you must suspend your entrenched disbelief in order to see what actually is right before you, Darby."

"There are no catamounts with us today," I declared with confidence.

"I wouldn't be so sure," Silas replied, looking closely at the window. "Sometimes you just have to know where to look."

"What do you mean?" Emily asked. She was growing more curious as she watched Silas examine the tomb's window.

"If you are struggling to find what you seek on Earth, sometimes you just have to raise your eyes to heaven to find enlightenment."

Emily and I joined Silas at the window to see what had caught his attention. Standing on a stone block, his nose was mere inches from the glass. Turning, he looked at us and smiled.

"What is it?" I asked.

"Divine intervention. I give you the catamount and bear." He stepped off the stone block and pointed to the glowing heavens in the painted window.

Emily and I took his place to get a better look at the window canvas. Neither one of us saw anything resembling an eastern mountain lion or a bear.

"Where? I don't see any animals," I said, growing annoyed with his trickery.

"See the support bar on the right side of the window? Follow it up to the first large cloud. Now move to the left and you should see the head of a bear in the cloud."

"Oh my God," Emily said in disbelief, "but where's the catamount?"

"From the bear's head, move upward to the left at a diagonal. See the blue space in the dark cloud? The elusive catamount head is hiding there."

"I'll be damned," I said, feeling foolish that I had doubted Silas once again. "That's incredible."

"Not really," Silas said while dabbing his brow with his handkerchief.

"You knew it was there?" I asked.

"I suspected it."

"Why?" I pressed.

"Painters have been hiding animals in their artworks for hundreds of years. Secret images can be found in many of the great works of Renaissance painters. Titian, Rafael, and even Leonardo da Vinci were masters at hiding things in plain sight. To see the unseen, all you need is the right perspective. For example, did you know if you turn the Mona Lisa on its side, you can find the heads of a buffalo, an ape, and a lion floating in the air?"

"What in the world are you talking about?" I asked, bewildered.

"Envy," he answered.

"Envy?"

"Did I stutter? Yes, envy you jackass! In addition, if you look at the Mona Lisa at a forty-five-degree angle, there's a serpent coming out of her heart."

"I still don't get it," I said, giving up and returning my focus to the window.

"Leonardo wrote cryptically in his journal about how to paint envy. He said, 'Make her heart gnawed by a swelling serpent... Give her a leopard's skin, because this creature kills the lion out of envy.' It appears crystal clear to me that Leo was envious of Francesco del Giocondo."

"Okay, now you lost me too," Emily said, shaking her head.

Silas let out a deep sigh before continuing. "I'll go real slow for you two Ivy League graduates, so pay attention please. The Mona Lisa is also called 'La Gioconda' which means 'the jolly lady' in Italian. La Gioconda is also a play on Francisco del Giocondo's last name. The model for the Mona Lisa was Giocondo's wife. Leo was smitten with her. So he hides the images of the lion and snake and other animals in the painting to represent his own envy of Giocondo. Leo was lusting for Mona."

"Yeah…she's was a real looker," I announced over my shoulder.

"Beauty is in the eye of the beholder," Emily shot back.

"The point is that you can't always spell things out. The hidden images in our window here are clues to help us find the answers we seek."

"So what do we do next?" I asked.

"We listen to the riddle and follow the catamount and the bear."

"Simple," I said in jest.

"It really is simple," Silas responded. "The riddle tells us to *follow the Catamount and Bear oblique*. The word oblique means slanting or diagonal. If we look closely at the painted window here, the two animals in the clouds are askew of one another. If we draw an imaginary line through the animals—"

"We have our diagonal line," I said, finally understanding Silas' thinking.

"Yes, and if we follow that diagonal line all the way down to where it touches the ground—"

"We find what? The location of the Pit of Hell?" Emily asked.

145

"We find our answers, Ms. Baines. Good or bad, our quest ends here," Silas said, pointing to the intersection of the oblique and the ground.

"Then it looks like our next stop is Crawford Notch," I observed.

"Or the mountains bordering it, my dear boy," Silas added.

Emily's face turned ashen as she stared at the painted window, her eyes following the imaginary diagonal to the ground. Mount Webster and Thoreau Falls lurked in this area, the location of her most harrowing teenage experience. I learned later that it was a place of horror for her, a true pit of hell. The experience seemed to come crashing back into her consciousness despite decades spent trying to irradiate the violation. After several moments, her feet grew heavy and her legs buckled. She didn't speak. Darkness was closing in around her as she hit the ground while Silas and I scrambled to catch her.

Silas was cradling her head as I fluttered around her, checking her breathing and her heart rate, as Emily regained consciousness. She was alive, but probably preferred the alternative at this point.

"What in the world happened?" I asked.

"I fainted," she hissed at me, "and why are you touching me?"

"We thought you were dead. I was just trying to check your vitals."

"I don't need any man checking my anything," she roared, "so stop touching me!"

"Try to relax... You're in shock. Your organs and tissues weren't getting enough oxygen. You passed out and hit your head on the ground. If I weren't a trained medic, you'd probably be dead by now. You can thank me later."

Surely, Emily's entire body was hurt, her head pulsating in excruciating pain. The pain clawed at her eyes, making her vision blurry while her jaw clenched shut. She couldn't stand up on her own and must have felt just as helpless as she did on that putrid summer day so long ago. Emily cursed at herself for being so weak. She thought this was all behind her and that she could control it. She began to convulse, giant sobs that made it difficult for her to catch her breath.

"We need to get her to a hospital, Silas. I'll carry her, you go pull the car around to the back."

"Will she be OK?" Silas asked.

"I hope so, but she needs to be checked out at an emergency room as soon as possible. They'll be able to tell us more."

Silas lifted Emily into a sitting position and then left the crypt at a jog, heading back the way we had come earlier. Emily's eyes remained closed but she managed to subdue her weeping. The color returned to her face as I supported her in my arms.

"I'm going to carry you," I told her.

"I can walk on my own, thank you very much. I don't need you helping me," she said through eyes now half open.

"Why are you angry with me? I'm just trying to help you."

"I don't need your help or anyone else's. I just want to be left alone. It was so stupid of me to come back here. I was comfortable in my life. I don't need this," she said, rising to her feet.

"What's going on, Emily? It looks like you had an anxiety attack. Talk to me."

"I've had them before but none recently. Something about that window brought back some bad memories I've been trying to forget. I can't do this anymore, Darby. I'm going back home to New York."

"You can go wherever you want after we get you to the hospital. You knocked your head pretty good. You might have a concussion."

"Then let's go. I don't want to waste another minute here with you."

"As you wish," was all I could say as I glanced one last time at the window into the past, then we walked out of the crypt door and into an uncertain future.

Emily's sudden desire to leave left me numb. As much as I fought it, I liked having her around. I had stupidly let her back into my heart only to see her leave me once again for no reason at all.

***

Pickford Marsh listened with contempt to the voice on the other end of the phone without saying a single word. He learned that Darby Weeks had made more progress in three days than the man thought possible. The Stickney heir now posed an imminent threat to all that Pickford coveted. Now, drastic measures were needed to ensure Darby Weeks did not complete his journey home. If Pickford failed, all would be lost. The instructions from the voice were clear. When the call ended, Pickford buzzed his secretary.

"Get a hold of Giselle," he said. "I need her to clean up this mess once and for all."

CHAPTER 14

Emily exited the hospital and climbed into the waiting car, relieved to be heading back to the city. She had been trapped in a sterile room for the past two days while men in white coats poked and prodded at her. She realized that it had been a mistake to return to Bretton Woods. Despite all of her financial means, she couldn't buy back what was lost long ago or keep bottled up the suppressed terrors she had worked so hard to erase. Upon returning to the city, Emily would bury herself back into her work and forget about all the grudges and deceptions that lingered in the North Country. She suppressed a laugh, remembering what Oscar Wilde had said about deception and love. '*Deceiving others. That is what the world calls a romance.*' Based on his definition, all her relationships must have been epic love affairs.

Closing her eyes, Emily relaxed in the backseat of the car as the driver left the hospital grounds and began the three-hour journey back to civilization. She would use this time alone to wipe clean the memories of the past few days. She no longer cared for that part of her life. She was eager to move forward and never look back. The sound of car doors locking shut interrupted her thoughts. Opening her eyes, she realized that they were heading in the wrong direction, back to the north instead of south toward New York City.

"Driver, I think you're lost," Emily said with annoyance. "We're going in the wrong direction." She hated incompetence.

"Oh no, I'm quite sure we're going in the right direction," Pickford Marsh cackled, removing his cap and flashing a hideous smile into the rearview mirror that soon vanished behind the closing privacy glass. Trapped again, Emily's nightmare was just beginning.

***

Silas and I left the hospital with reluctance after hearing Emily was going to be fine. Her nasty fall left her concussed and irritable with a piercing headache. Refusing to speak to me, Emily had made arrangements to return to New York via a private car service. The doctors told her that time would heal her ailments, but she needed to rest and returning to New York would at least make her more comfortable. Neither Silas nor I understood at the time what caused the episode at the tomb or Emily's even more bizarre mood change, but there was little else we could do for her. We decided to return to Bretton Woods. Armed with the general knowledge of where to look, we now only had to figure out what we were looking for out in the wilderness. This was no easy task. The riddle referred to the *pit of hell* and *a well of lost souls*, but what that actually meant or looked like on the ground was anyone's guess. Would we find fire and brimstone at that intersection between heaven and Earth, or something worse? There was only one way to find out.

Departing New Hampshire's capital city, we headed north—passing once again through the southern chokehold of the notches—and reentered the North Country. After several days of traipsing through libraries and graveyards, I welcomed a return to what I was starting to think of as home again. Seeing the bone-white, red roofed structure once again released a tension that had been winding up inside of me. Emily's latest exit from my life had caused all the anxiety and feelings of inadequacy to come crashing back. As much as I might have resented Emily's unexpected return to my life, her presence over the past few days had helped soothed many of the freshly reopened wounds associated with my homecoming.

The Peugeot rumbled up to the front entrance of the hotel and slid under the portico. The two valets on duty looked at one another as if playing out a silent game of Ro-Sham-Bo to see who would have to endure the bombastic lecture associated with parking Silas' car.

"Now boys," Silas began, "this car is what you might call an antique. It's older than the both of you combined. I would like it washed, waxed, and then returned to the storage barn and covered post haste. And don't even think about taking it for a joyride because I already wrote down the mileage."

Having just spent what felt like an eternity with Silas, I appreciated his chiding being directed at someone else for a change. Climbing the steps and entering the lobby, the smell of freshly brewed coffee and delectable oatmeal raisin cookies filled the air. The caffeine and sugar did wonders for my mood, giving me a second wind. I filled my pockets with the still-warm cookies and savored my coffee while wandering down the expansive lobby. Stopping outside the historic Gold Room, I read the bronzed plaque affixed to its door.

> *In this room the articles of agreement*
> *setting up the International Monetary Fund*
> *were signed in July, 1944.*

The simplicity of the sign seemed too understated to me considering the enormity of the historical event. This hotel had hosted great men and even finer women. In just twenty-two days, seven hundred and thirty-four delegates from forty-four Allied nations reshaped the western world, fueling a post-war economic juggernaut, and all they got was this little bronze plaque. I did much less and was showered with the country's highest honor. Where was the sense in that?

Pushing open the door, I gazed into the meeting room looking for something but was only greeted by silence. The echoes of the past were deafening. Taking a seat at the massive circular oak table, I tried to imagine the expectations and pressure felt by each of the seven hundred and thirty-four delegates. How did they go about rebuilding the world in just three weeks? I couldn't even *begin* to rebuild my life in three months. I lacked the necessary focus and motivation. The riddle lit a spark in me that grew into a glowing ember, but my curious reaction to Emily's hasty departure nearly extinguished it again. *Why did I come back here?*

Quinn poked his head into the empty room, interrupting my self-disparaging moment. "I see you're meeting with your fan club."

"Shouldn't you be handing out jaywalking tickets or something?" I shot back.

"Welcome back, Darby," he said with a laugh. "How was the trip?"

"Let's see… I was nearly asphyxiated in a French roadster, I confessed to stealing a literary treasure when I was seven, and I communed with the founding fathers of the transcendental movement."

"Sounds like a hell of vacation."

"Oh, and we've just about solved all the riddles."

"Really? Pray tell," Quinn asked, slipping back into investigator mode.

I exhaled, starting to feel weak again. "Where do I begin? I really need to process everything first. Maybe I can catch up with you over dinner?"

"It's your lucky day, I've already made reservations with Flavio. Seven work?"

The last thing I wanted to do was walk the dining-room gauntlet again, but perhaps having already made his point, Flavio would be a little more discreet this time around.

"Seven would be great. I'll see you then," I said with a wave.

"OK, but you have to tell me everything. No holding back," Quinn said before quickly exiting the room.

After Quinn had left, I realized I forgot to ask him about Father Callaghan's death. Where were they with the investigation? It could wait. I was sure I'd find out tonight. My immediate concerns were more pressing; my body was craving sleep and I needed a shower.

Leaving the Gold Room, I zigzagged to the right, intent on climbing the back stairs up to the apartment, but I exited out onto the veranda instead. I was being pulled by something, drawn to a spot that held the clues to everything. I drifted toward the South Porch again and gazed out toward the east. Crawford Notch etched the sky in the distance, beckoning me. A cloudless blue sky filled the horizon. In my mind, I superimposed the painted window of Stickney's tomb onto nature's canvas laid out before me. I could see the catamount and the bear hovering in the heavens. I followed the invisible diagonal down to where it touched the earth. Whatever answers were yearning to be found, they would be discovered somewhere around Mount Webster. I just didn't know if I had the desire to find them anymore.

Sensing I was being watched, I glanced down at the service road below me. Staring back were the imposing gray eyes of Finnegan Doyle.

"What do you want?" I shouted down to him.

"See you tonight," he replied, pretending his finger was a gun.

"No can do, I have a dinner date."

"Yes, you do." He laughed before disappearing into the bowels of the hotel below me.

***

Sweat beaded on my forehead ten hours later as I marched toward the main dining room. The bustle of the lobby seemed to momentarily ebb as I passed by. The sound of my stiff corfam shoes flexing and this crisp uniform with the medal strangling my neck once again caused stares. It hypnotized the throngs of tourists who had gathered in the grand hallway awaiting their evening activities to commence. I passed the guest check-in desk, reaching a confluence of three paths. Looking once again down the left hallway, my eyes lifted to meet those on the portrait of the princess. She stared down at me from her high judgmental perch. *Do you still believe in me?*

Since returning to Bretton Woods for the second time, I'd been waiting for a spark to reignite inside me, some sort of urgency to complete the journey that I had started alone and then with Emily and Silas by my side, but I still felt nothing. Was it apathy, fear or something worse? I tried to figure it out in my head. The princess offered me no help.

Gazing down the dining room hallway, I spotted Flavio hovering over his coveted reservation book. He looked up, appearing to sense my presence, as his eyes zeroed in on me.

"My vision must surely deceive me," he said while playfully rubbing his eyes with his balled fists. "What a pleasant surprise! You honor my dining room with your presence once again, my friend."

"Please, no fuss is necessary *amico mio*, my friend," I replied closing the distance between us and feeling embarrassed by the scene he was beginning to make. The dining room's strict formal attire policy, forced me to wear my Navy uniform once again.

"No fuss, you say? One makes a fuss for a man of your courage and mettle. You do me an honor by allowing me to praise you, Senior Chief."

I nodded, understanding Flavio's need to celebrate my accomplishments. While I still found the attention unsettling, I was learning to tolerate it by convincing myself that people were honoring and showing respect not to me per se, but to the medal and what it stood for.

"Whom are you dining with tonight?" Flavio inquired.

"Quinn Matthews," I said. I looked over Flavio's shoulder, trying to spot him in the dining room.

Flavio frowned at me and said, "Unfortunately our chief of hotel security is indisposed at the moment. I regret to inform you that he won't be able to join you tonight."

I swore under my breath, wondering why no one could keep a damn appointment in this hotel. "I assume you have someone else in mind that I could join for dinner or drinks?"

"Most certainly." He flashed an executioner's smile. "He's waiting in the Princess Lounge now. Please follow me, Senior Chief."

We snaked a path through the crowded bar in the Princess lounge. Heads turned as black-tied revelers and prim socialites offered compliments while they waited for their tables. I acknowledged the presence of the well-wishers as I scanned the room wondering who I would be stuck with tonight. Flavio pulled open the thick curtain that shielded the lounge's private seating area in the back, and I just about keeled over when I saw my dining companion for the evening.

"Where the hell have you been???" croaked the raspy voice of Father Callaghan.

I stood there in shock looking at him with my mouth agape. "Oh my God, I thought you were dead."

"I'm very much in the land of the living, thank you," he replied blowing smoke from his Macanudo up into my face. "Are you just gonna stand there catching flies with your mouth open or are you gonna to sit down and join me for a drink?"

I took a seat on the couch next to him and ordered my usual drink, still not believing Father Callaghan was alive and sitting in front of me. "What about all the blood in the chapel?"

"I cut myself shaving," he joked, taking a sip of his Ginko Pinko.

The waitress arrived with my witch hazel-infused iced gimlet. Reaching for it, I downed the drink in one motion then ordered two more. The slow burn of the vodka jolted me out of my dazed stupor. "You were missing for days. We thought the worst. What in the world happened to you?"

"Well I just told my story to Quinn. He left to call the FBI and the local authorities. They're still trying to figure out who was murdered and where the other body went," Callaghan said.

I craved more details. "What other body?"

"The one I saw slayed in the Ammonoosuc River by two men. They tried to kill me too, but I made it to the chapel and locked myself in before they could finish the job."

"Were you shot with a gun?" I asked, looking at the gauzed bandages engulfing his leg.

"From your mouth to God's ear I wish I was, but the bastards put a crossbow arrow into my thigh instead. Worst pain I ever felt and that's saying something since I've been bayonetted by the Viet Cong. Thanks to Comrade Charlie, I've had a steel plate in there since Nam. I probably would have bled out by the time I regain consciousness if it wasn't for that plate and my guardian angel."

"Whoa, whoa, whoa...slow down a minute and rewind," I said wanting to fully understand what had transpired that night. "Start from the beginning. A couple of nights earlier you told me to study the cicada. What's happened since then?"

"On the night I was attacked, I did what I always do when the weather is nice – I walked home from the hotel to the chapel under heaven's divine splendor. There was quite a crowd outside that night…drinking and cavorting…so I shadowed the river down past the clubhouse since I was 'more sail than ballast' if you know what I mean." He gave me a wink and then knocked back the remains of his drink. "I was just about to ford the river over to the chapel side when I came across a group of people in the river. They were struggling to lift someone out of the water. I shouted and asked them if they needed any help. I painted them with my Maglite and that's when I realized they weren't Christians. I saw the face of a dead man bluer than a Jazz club. One of the two assailants had just cut the arm off the corpse. The tendons were all hanging out loose. It looked like they were in the process of hacking the body apart in the darkness of the river."

While the demonic image that Father Callaghan so gruesomely described should have repulsed me, my own experience as a Navy Corpsman had desensitized me to such horrors. I had seen much worse in the battles of Fallujah and the arid tribal lands of Afghanistan.

"Was there any blood spurting out around the arm or the shoulder socket?" I asked, my brain methodically going through a trauma checklist.

"What kind of damn question is that to ask?"

"Sorry, Father. It's an ingrained habit related to triage. I was trying to deduce how long the victim had been dead."

"I didn't hang around long enough to get a good look since one of the perpetrators rushed toward me and I hightailed it to the opposite bank. As I exited the water, an arrow pierced my leg. Everything happened pretty fast after that. I remember stumbling through the trees, snapping branches off, and then I was in the chapel. I tried to bolt the door, but my hands wouldn't work. I took a few steps and then fell down. The last thing I saw was the face of a guardian angel."

"Gabriel?" I guessed.

"No, Finnegan Doyle."

"Finn?" I asked, thinking I'd misheard him.

"If it wasn't for that boy I would have died for sure. He tied a tourniquet to my leg and carried me to safety. Apparently, he squirreled me away somewhere until I had stabilized and then got me to a hospital."

"Why didn't Finn get help immediately?" I asked.

"I believe he was afraid of being wrongly accused by people like you and me. I can't believe that I'm saying this, Darby, but I was wrong about Finn. His heart is in the right place. It's just his methods that I sometimes question."

"Finn?" I repeated, still not believing he saved Father Callaghan. "How did he happen to be near the chapel that night?"

"I don't know. Why don't you ask him yourself," he said as Finnegan parted the curtain and sat down in the seat across from me.

"Good to see you again, Darbs. Are you confessing your sins?"

"I was just about to ask you the same thing." I felt my hackles begin to rise. "Father Callaghan was telling me how you saved him at the chapel. It's quite a coincidence that you just happened to be there to save the day."

"Yes it was and I'd appreciate it if you didn't prejudge me. If you remember, I cautioned you earlier in the woods that things are not always as they seem. So be careful when picking sides."

"Then answer my question and tell us how you happened to be at the chapel that night," I pressed.

"I had my reasons, you'll just have to trust that my intentions were good."

"I don't trust anyone who pulls a knife on me," I replied.

"Finn, did you pulled a knife on Darby? That's not a very Christian thing to do."

"Would you have preferred it if I'd thrown him to the lions, Padre?" Finn joked. "He provoked me on purpose and I was just putting an end to our conversation."

Callaghan puffed away on his cigar, pondering the situation. "Both you shut the hell up and listen to me. The three of us need to quickly find a way to work together and trust one another otherwise I fear we'll all end up dead like that poor bastard in the river. I propose we treat tonight's dinner conversation as a twisted confession booth. We share what we know and we keep each other's secrets, no matter what they may be."

"I'm game if Darby agrees to it as well," Finn answered.

I thought about the inherent risks of revealing all I knew to them, but my curiosity surrounding Father Callaghan's disappearance, Finn's role in it, and the riddles that led me all over New England convinced me to play along, at least temporarily.

"Okay, I'll agree to this proposal on one condition. No one else can know what we say to each other tonight...not Quinn, not the county sheriff, and not the FBI."

Everyone nodded in agreement as we toasted our triple alliance. "Okay, Finn, you start. How did you happen to be at the chapel that night and what did you see and hear?"

Finn stared at me for a long moment trying to decide if I would keep my word. I knew that if I broke our agreement, he wouldn't rest until he hunted me down and killed me. He could believe his secrets were safe with me.

"Go on, Finn. I'm a priest. Our conversations are considered confidential and private under the clergy–penitent privilege. Nothing you say before me is admissible in a court of law."

Finn took a long sip of his drink and then exhaled through his teeth before beginning.

"I've been following some of Pickford Marsh's henchmen, Aqua-Nord employees, for several months now. I've sat back feeling helpless as they cleared the forests, dug holes in the ground, and tried to pressure the local town councils in order to get their right-of-way permits expedited and approved. I was following two of these men the night of the murder. They were at the hotel during the opening night of the Great Gatsby weekend. Initially I thought they were just there to enjoy themselves, but I found it odd that neither of them was drinking nor participating in any of the festivities."

"What were they doing then?" I asked.

"Watching and waiting. They were trailing a man. They watched him as he ordered a beer and then followed him down towards to the river. A third employee, a woman who I've seen before at Aqua-Nord events, was dressed as a banquet server. She offered him some food and then entered a waiting car and quickly left. I suspect the food was poisoned because the man fell ill shortly thereafter and then collapsed into the river."

"What did the two Aqua-Nord goons do when the man fell into the river?" I asked, prompting Finn to continue with the story.

161

Finn closed his eyes, replaying the events in his mind. He didn't want to relive what he witnessed.

"Finn, it's OK. Go on now," Father Callaghan said.

"It had started to get dark and it was hard to see, but from my vantage point on top of the hotel's conference center roof, I could just make out the dark shape of the man as he floated downstream. He appeared to be face down and very dead. Pickford's two thugs just leisurely kept pace on shore with the body as the current carried it into the forest."

"You just sat there watching? You didn't get help or yell out and sound an alarm?" I asked.

"I didn't know what to do. I couldn't call the police since they were already looking for me so I left the roof and shadowed the two men into the woods."

"I must have been right behind you since it was nearly dark when I got to the edge of the river," Father Callaghan added. "What happened once you got in to the woods?"

"I crossed over the golf cart bridge by the clubhouse and began creeping along the river's edge on the opposite shore. I didn't want to chance running into the two goons in case they turned around and walked back toward the hotel. It was completely dark now, but the clear sky and rising moon gave me just enough light to see a little bit downstream."

"Could you see the two men?" I asked.

"Not at first. I kept looking for them on the opposite shore, but it wasn't until I rounded the bend in the river that I heard them in the water and then I actually saw them."

"Tell me what you saw," Callaghan demanded.

Finn was noticeably shaken. He downed a shot of Van Gogh Blue Vodka before continuing.

"They were both standing in the river up to their waists trying to free the body which had become entangled in some downed trees. They were cursing because they couldn't get it free. I moved a little further down the shore to get a better look. The moonlight was reflecting off the water and I could see one of the men was holding a large knife. He began to hack away at the dead man's arm, trying to free it from the branches. I threw up at the sight. I couldn't watch the butchering that had commenced. I started to backtrack. I was veering away from the riverbank when I spotted the illuminated chapel tower peeking out above the trees. I decided to make my way there and appeal to God while I waited them out. I was surprised when I heard Father Callaghan call out to the men and then I heard him scream. Father Callaghan emerged from the trees. He was making a hell of a racket. I followed him into the chapel and bolted the door behind me."

"And shortly after that I saw you hovering over me, just before I passed out," Father Callaghan added.

"Did the two men follow you to the chapel?" I asked.

"A little bit later, I heard what sounded like someone outside trying the latches on all the doors as I was applying a tourniquet to Father Callaghan's leg. I assume they were searching for him."

"Father, do you think they knew who you were?" I asked.

"It's possible, but I doubt it. Butchers like that usually aren't church-goers."

"You'd be surprised," I said.

"They didn't try to force themselves into the chapel so they probably figured you were hiding somewhere in the woods," Finn suggested.

"They also had a body still in the river that they had to dispose of before sunrise," I said, "so I doubt they were going to waste too much time scouring the woods for the witness to their crime. You weren't the primary target, Father. I wonder who the poor guy was that they killed?"

Finn stared down at the floor. "I can tell you exactly who the guy was." Both Father Callaghan and I looked at Finn waiting for him to name the victim. "It was Jacques Robarge," Finn said in a barely audible whisper.

"What???" Father Callaghan said surprised. "Jacques was Aqua-Nord's mouthpiece for its Granite Pass project. He was one of their most valuable employees, or so I thought. Why in the world would they want to kill him?"

"Maybe his value had diminished?" I said. "The newspapers have been full of stories about all the delays and difficulties Aqua-Nord has been having with the local town planning boards. Perhaps Pickford Marsh lost patience with Mr. Jacques Robarge?"

"So why have him killed? Couldn't they have just fired him?" Father Callaghan suggested.

Finn shook his head before he offered his take on the situation. "Jacques Robarge was a long-term employee of Aqua-Nord. He was a results man and Pickford Marsh considered him a valuable asset and a personal confidant. The only reason I can see that he would be killed would be if Jacques finally had enough of the Aqua-Nord machine and wanted out. We all know how despicable Pickford Marsh can be. Just imagine what secrets his right-hand man would know. Jacques would be a serious threat if he ever decided to leave the company."

"So they butcher him in the river just a stone's throw away from the hotel during one of the busiest weekends of the year and hope no one sees or hears anything? That seems a little too risky and amateurish for Pickford Marsh," I theorized.

"I agree," Finn said, "and Pickford Marsh has made a career out of eliminating headaches discretely by making them look like—" Finn's eyes met mine as he cut himself off mid-sentence.

"Accidents," I said.

"Darby, I'm sorry. I didn't mean to trivialize—"

I held up my hand, stopping his apology. "It's okay, Finn. There's no question in my mind that Pickford Marsh played a part in my father and grandfather's deaths. He's been obsessed with this long standing feud between our families for far too long and I'm sure nothing would give him more pleasure than killing me as well and ending any perceived threat that I or my family might present to him."

"No offense, Darby," Father Callaghan began, "but I can't believe Pickford Marsh would waste a single minute on you. He's worth billions of dollars and hardly ever goes out in public. It seems to me that he has been focusing all of his energy on that ill-fated Granite Pass project. You haven't been around in almost twenty years and the last time I checked, you're unemployed. How are you any sort of threat to him?"

"Simple," I said. "I'm a Stickney and thanks to you, Father, I also know where to look for the source of his fear."

"What do you mean, Darby?" Finn asked.

I looked at Finn. "A couple of nights before Father Callaghan was attacked, we had drinks in the dinning room of the hotel. Do you remember what you told me, Father?"

"I told you to study the cicada. That it would put you on the path to discovery."

"Yes. So the next morning I examined the decapitated insect a little closer and found a rolled-up piece of parchment hidden inside the exoskeleton. Written on that paper was a riddle that helped me find two additional riddles. These riddles combined sent me on a wild goose chase all over New England."

"And what did you discover?" Finn asked.

"That I should have read more classical literature," I quipped.

Finn stared at me with a blank look on his face. He obviously lacked any sense of humor.

"I ended up at the tomb of Joseph Stickney," I continued.

"I knew it!" shouted Father Callaghan.

"The final riddle told me to find the view that would lead to the *pit of hell and a well of lost souls.*"

"Did you find the view?" Finn asked.

"We did. There was a single painted window in Stickney's tomb that replicated the view from the hotel's South Porch. Some additional clues indicated that what we were seeking could be found somewhere in the Crawford Notch area close to Mount Webster."

The color drained from Finn's face as a sudden revelation struck him. "You don't mean some place like Thoreau Falls?" he asked.

The mention of Thoreau's name sent bolts of electricity cascading through my body. It couldn't be a coincidence. That had to be the place where we would find our answers. "What would make you think about that place?" I asked cautiously, not wanting to reveal my excitement.

"After I put the tourniquet on Callaghan's leg, I tried to think of some place I could evacuate us to where we would be safe and where I would have some time to think through my next moves. I decided to take Father Callaghan up to the Zealand Falls hut. This time of year it doesn't get any foot traffic and it's just far enough to the south that no one would see any smoke from the burning wood stove."

"If you were holed up at the hut with Father Callaghan, how did you end up at Thoreau Falls?" I asked.

"Father Callaghan was feeling better the next morning. He had regained consciousness so I went out scouting near Thoreau Falls. I was getting ready to make my way back to the hut when the same two Aqua-Nord goons rode in unexpectedly on ATVs. Initially I thought they had somehow tracked me, but they were in the area for another reason," he said, closing his eyes again.

"That's a pretty isolated spot this time of year. If they weren't tracking you, why would they be that far from the main road or the hotel?"

"They arrived a little before sunset and were carrying two large duffle bags on the sides of their ATVs. They dismounted their vehicles and quickly trekked off, each shouldering one of the duffle bags. I waited there hiding…thinking they would be back in a half hour at most since the sun was going down. They didn't return until sunrise the next day. They no longer had their duffle bags with them. They headed off quickly, driving deeper into the forest."

"Did they camp out somewhere?" I asked.

"I thought they had at first and then I explored the downslope area where they had headed with the bags. I didn't find any campsite, no fire pit, no signs that they were even there."

"You found nothing?" I pressed.

Finn closed his eyes once more. I could see he was holding something back.

"Tell him, Finn," Father Callaghan urged.

Finn exhaled loudly through his teeth again. "I did find two things – a pack of French cigarettes and the remains of a human ear. I think the butchers put the pieces of Jacques Robarge into those two duffle bags and then discarded him somewhere around Thoreau Falls."

"All you found was an ear? No other body parts or blood stains?" I asked.

"Nothing else, it was like the ground just swallowed him up without a trace."

"The *Pit of Hell* and the *Well of Lost Souls*," I muttered to myself.

"You think those riddles reference the area around Thoreau Falls?" Father Callaghan asked me.

"I don't believe in coincidences. The answers we seek have to be in that area." I recited the last poem out loud again,

> '*Follow the Catamount and Bear oblique*
> *To uncover the past, the truth will reek.*
> *The pit of hell, a well of lost souls*
> *Justice be swift, the names extolled.*'

"Damn," Finn said, "that place doesn't sound pleasant at all."

"Given what we know about the end of Jacques Robarge, I'm starting to think it might be where the Marsh family hides all its skeletons…literally."

"And to think, most of us only have a closet," Father Callaghan mused.

168

"I propose we reconnoiter the area, turn over every leaf and look behind every rock until we find something that's out of place. Pickford Marsh is hiding his secrets somewhere out there and I'm going to find them." I was determined to find out what had happened to my own family.

"Darby," Finn responded, "I have already been through every nook and cranny up there. There's nothing to be found. The weather's supposed to turn bad tomorrow. The forecasters are predicting that we'll get our first snowfall of the season. I think it would be better to wait and use the snowfall to our advantage."

"How do we do that?" I asked.

"It's off season," Finn continued. "I don't expect that we'll get too many hikers up there until next spring. Let me watch the area. The snow will record the tracks of anyone who transits in or out."

"And what if no one returns until spring? The snow will be gone by then."

"Then we can always use some bait and just wait patiently like anglers tempting fish to take a bite."

I considered Finn's plan and knew it probably was our best bet. There were just too many acres of wilderness surrounding Thoreau Falls to practically search it all. At the same time, I kept hearing Thoreau's words rattling around inside my head. *'Many men go fishing all their lives without knowing that it is not fish they are after.'* What was it that I was seeking? Was it closure related to my family or vengeance for an ancient enemy that I had been raised to hate?

"Okay, we'll cast our line and watch and wait, no matter how long it takes."

CHAPTER 15

I waited restlessly through the ill winds of a muted autumn and then watched as the bitter snows fell through the earliest of winters. Doing nothing was the hardest part. I felt like a castaway marooned on a lavish island with butler service. The monochromatic darkness of winter mirrored my own emotional state. I grew hopeless, doubting I would ever get the elusive answers that I yearned for most of my life.

While I waited, thoughts of Emily turned over in my brain. I wondered if she was doing well. I resisted the temptation to call and hear her voice again. She chose to leave and made it clear that our past should remain in the past. She said there was no future for us. We had nothing in common anymore except the town that we used to call home. I had stayed far longer in

Bretton Woods than I ever intended to and every day I wondered why I just didn't pack up and leave for good for the second and final time and never look back. I had no family. I had no real friends anymore. I had nothing except an inheritance and a family name that had weighed me down for far too long. The cursed medal only added to my burden. I looked out the window of the Rosebrook Bar and pondered my future.

"The last time I saw wind like that I was caught up in a *derecho* at the summit of our little mountain," Silas said as he sat down next to me and gazed out at the wind-whipped snow blowing off the summit of Mount Washington and the other peaks of the Presidential Range. "It struck in the pre-dawn hours of July 5th, 1999."

It was like listening to the History Channel or some NPR show except the host never gets a word in. Unfortunately I could not turn the channel.

"I awoke at three in the morning, unable to sleep because of the stagnant air inside my tent. I went outside for an early morning stroll to get some relieve from the blasted heat when I spied an immense electrical storm brewing to the Northwest. A huge storm was blowing in and I realized that I had picked the wrong place to pitch my tent for the night. I broke camp and hightailed it over to the weather observatory thinking I could shelter in there until the danger passed."

"You do realize that camping is not allowed anywhere on top of the summit?" I asked. "You could have been ticketed by a park ranger."

Silas looked at me harshly for interrupting the flow of his story. Then he just continued. "I banged on the door of the Sherman Adams building for a good five minutes as the winds

171

roared up the mountain and a multitude of lightning strikes rolled their way towards me like a German Blitzkrieg."

"Did they let you in?"

"The door finally did open to my relief as a woman smiled at me. She stared at me with wicked eyes and then shut the door on me, locking me out and refusing me entry. Turning around, I could see the shelf cloud of the storm illuminated by massive internal lightning as it rose up over the slope, roaring like a vengeful god looking for a sacrifice." Silas paused for a long moment while looking out the window, at the wisps of blowing snow that were forming mares' tails high over the mountain peaks. His silence was unsettling. As much as I wanted to be left alone, Silas' story had sucked me in and I needed to know how it ended.

"Tell me, Silas, how did you survive the storm?"

"I made a desperate sprint up the stairs and into the stonewalled Tip Top House. The storm assaulted the building for well over a half an hour with ninety mile-per-hour winds and forks of lightning so fierce that they had to have been cast out from the very hand of Zeus. And then all was quiet. I thought death had finally come to me. I walked outside and looked up at the heavens, where the edges of Milky Way engulfed me. It was as close to the Creator that I have ever been in my life. Then I looked down toward the observatory and saw the green eyes of the devil looking back at me."

"The woman? The same one who tried to kill you?" I asked.

"The Green Monster herself looking dejected that I had survived her death trap."

"Wait, you don't mean—?"

172

"Yes, I do. It was Elsie Fitzgerald in the flesh," he announced.

"Why in the world would she want you dead?" I asked, trying to figure out if this was just another imaginary tale.

"She is of the Marsh clan. As wicked as they come."

"What? Her parents were from Germany. She's not a Marsh," I replied.

"In the North Country, the old families have always had to choose sides, Darby. They align themselves for protection or for favors. Some support the Stickney clan and some subjugate themselves to the Marsh bloodline."

"That's ridiculous," I said. "Why would anyone want to be associated with Pickford Marsh and his family?"

"Because some have no choice and some have no soul," he said in a whisper.

I looked closely at Silas and noticed for the first time that he did not look well. A veil of seriousness had fallen over his face as he continued to stare up at the ridgelines.

"Silas, is everything all right?"

"I'm getting old Darby, too old for secrets," he said, looking into my eyes. "It's about time that you learned the truth about you and me."

"What are you talking about...what secrets?"

"For starters, everything I've told you—every story, every personal anecdote, and every memory—has been the absolute truth. I have never lied to you, but I've never told you the whole truth either."

"Why not?" I asked, not knowing what else to say.

Silas breathed heavily through his nose. He was thinking through his next sentence with care. "When you were born, it

173

was decided for your own protection that you should be raised as a Weeks and not as a Stickney."

"I already knew that," I said, growing impatient.

"But what you don't know is that Horatio and I had another brother. That evil mongrel Pickford Marsh killed him, but he had a son. This nephew of ours went on to marry and produced another son, our great nephew. That boy had a very troubled and challenging childhood. He felt lost and overwhelmed in the uncertain and high profile world of Bretton Woods. He put immense pressure on himself to live up to some imaginary family legacy. Horatio and I looked on, feeling helpless since we were forbidden to interfere or even identify ourselves as blood relatives of the boy. Eventually our great nephew was driven from the North Country by subterfuge hatched up by his father's and grandfather's killer...Pickford Marsh."

I heard Silas' words, but refused to see what was right before me. I was tired of the lies. I was tired of feeling so alone. I was just plain tried.

"What are you trying to tell me, Silas?" I asked, seeking absolute clarity.

"What I'm trying to say is that I'm your great uncle. You, Horatio and I are all that is left of the Stickney bloodline. That fool Pickford thinks you are the last of the line, but we are three instead of one and we shall prevail in the end."

I looked out the window at the mountain whose dark shadow I had stood in for most of my life and saw a glimmer of light amongst the darkness. I wasn't alone anymore, but I had a long way to go before I could learn to appreciate my great uncle, the windbag.

"Is that it? No other deep family secrets?" I asked, feeling numb all over.

"Well since you asked, there is one more secret but it's very complicated. I think I should let you soak in what I've already told you before revealing the rest."

"How much more complicated can it get?" I honestly didn't believe anything he could tell me could shock me further.

"That, my grand nephew, depends on how well you know your European history," he said with a twinkle in his eye as he handed me a well-worn red leather-bound book. The volume felt substantial in my hand. Turning it over, I read the book's title.

"You've got to be kidding me? You're telling me that—"

"Indeed," was all Silas could say as he continued to look out at the mountain and worry.

***

Emily tried opening the doors. She tried kicking out the windows. She even tried to smash through the privacy glass that separated her from her abductor. Each one of her attempts was a waste of energy. She was trapped inside the speeding limo, heading north – back to Bretton Woods, back to her past. She hated enclosed spaces and was starting to panic. *What does he want with me?* She thought to herself. Emily barely knew the man. All of her previous encounters with Pickford Marsh had been brief and uneventful. A fake smile had always hid her fear of the man when she was in his presence. Darby's stories and his vitriol for the Marsh family had scared her senseless in the past. She wanted no part of their ancient feud.

Maybe Pickford found out about her prying into Aqua-Nord's affairs? The dirt she had dug up and the dots she had connected on her own could be a threat to his business affairs. But to kidnap her over that was ridiculous. He could have easily just paid her off like all the other victims Tither Publishing set their sights on.

"What do you want?" Emily screamed while she pounded her feet on the privacy glass. "Tell me what you want! Talk to me, goddamn it!" she yelled over and over again, but wretched silence was the only response she received from the driver as they crept closer to the North Country.

***

"Have you ever read Shakespeare?" Silas inquired as we reentered the lobby. We had just completed a brief stroll around the hotel's open-aired veranda.

"I attempted to a couple of times," I answered, shaking off the cold, "but I never could understand what the hell he was saying. The Old English was too confusing to me."

Silas sighed and mumbled to himself, "Youth, why do we even bother? Shakespeare wrote in Early Modern English not Old English so his language is just a generation away from what we use today."

"Please, I don't think I can handle a linguistic lecture at this moment."

"Fine, but please tell me that you have at least heard of *Romeo and Juliet?*"

"Of course," I huffed, "star-crossed lovers from two rival families who hated each other."

"That plot is rooted in the most basic of all human truths and it has played out an infinite number of times throughout recorded history. For example, the feud that currently exists right here in Bretton Woods between our family and the Marsh family actually goes back much further – way back to the old country of nobles and peasants."

176

"England?" I guessed.

"No, further East, to where the Gulf of Finland meets the Neva River," Silas corrected me.

"Pay no attention to his stories, Darby," Horatio interrupted. He was staring down Silas as he entered the room. "My brother is old and quite foolish."

"I did not see you standing there, dear brother," Silas said with some trepidation. "It is good to see you again. What are you doing back in Bretton Woods?"

"I bring news," Horatio continued. "Finnegan Doyle has spotted curious tracks in the snow and is investigating them as we speak. He will report back to us in the morning with what he finds, if anything."

"Good, maybe I can finally get some rest then," I said with a yawn. "I don't think I can handle any new information today."

"I suggest we all get some sleep. Tomorrow may be a long day." Horatio ushered me out of the room toward the elevator. As the lift doors began to close, I saw the two brothers turn to one another as if preparing to discuss something that they didn't want me to hear. There were obviously more secrets left to be discovered about my newfound family.

***

"What do you think you are doing, Silas?" Horatio asked after the elevator's door had closed.

"Telling the boy the truth. He needs to know everything. The days of sitting idly by and watching our brood suffer are over, dear brother. It's time to come out of hiding and fight for what is rightfully ours."

"I understand your frustration, Silas, but we are in the twilight of our lives while Darby still has half his life ahead of him, God willing. We cannot risk gambling away his future due to our own irritations about the past and the unfortunate turn of events."

"Horatio, calling the death of our brother and his only son an unfortunate turn of events diminishes both of their lives and their contributions to ours. They sacrificed themselves for us. Let us repay that debt by helping our great nephew attain what is rightfully his. Darby deserves to be told the truth and requires our guidance on what to do with it. He is the heir apparent. He is the one who will make things right again."

"I mourned the lost of our brother more than you'll ever know," Horatio said, "and I have beat down my own internal calls for vengeance more times then I can count. I am by nature cautious. Let us both sleep on this and wait until we hear back from Finnegan."

"I will honor your request tonight," Silas replied, "but I will not wait forever. Our days are numbered, brother, and we must see that the feud ends with the present generation. Pickford Marsh must finally be exposed for what he is, and he must be destroyed."

***

"Ms. Baines, you've been a naughty, naughty girl," Pickford Marsh said with a sneer. "Sticking your nose in where it doesn't belong. Don't you know not to rattle a hornet's nest?"

Emily struggled against the ropes that tied her to the chair in Pickford's office, but still replied with defiance. "I am by nature very curious, Mr. Marsh. For example, I find it interesting how Canadian regulators have just approved the application of a small pipeline company named Overbridge to reverse the flow of its pipeline. Correct me if I'm wrong, but this pipeline as I understand it currently carries crude oil, but with this new ruling it could conceivably carry tar sands from Alberta to Montreal."

"Why does this interest you?" Pickford asked. "Are you suddenly an energy enthusiast?"

"No, but imagine my surprise when I learned that Overbridge's parent company is none other than Aqua-Nord. I can connect the dots, Mr. Marsh. Aqua-Nord's top priority has been the acquisition of transmission rights for your Granite Pass project through Vermont, New Hampshire, and Maine. It would seem to me that if you can secure these transmission rights it is then only a matter of time before new pipelines are built and the Alberta tar sands start flowing from Montreal to Portland, Maine. How do you think local communities would react if they knew that toxic tar sands bitumen could be flowing through their pristine forests and across their crystal clear waterways?"

"I have enough troubles, Ms. Baines. I don't need anymore. What do you want?"

"It's funny how men like you only *count your troubles and never your happiness*," Emily replied. "I don't want anything except to see you exposed as the conniving scum that you really are."

"I can't help it," Pickford responded, "it's in my blood…and in yours. I am a descendent of Cossacks and even I can recognize your poorly quoted Dostoyevsky when I hear it. You are trouble and it will be the end of you."

"Well, I'm a girl," Emily said with a fake smile. "Trouble is all I know."

"Yes," Pickford said with a laugh, "and it has served you quite well. I've watched you with envy and pride, as Tither Publishing has grown from a grocery store rag into a global force

179

capable of taking down popes and false prophets. You strong-arm others and justify it by telling yourself that you are exposing hypocrisy. How noble of you."

"And you're any better, Mr. Marsh?"

"I do things for the most noble reason of all…to make money."

"To quote another Russian, 'I often think that men don't understand what is noble and what is ignorant, though they always talk about it.' Ignorance is your Achilles' heel. You'll self destruct and burn up like every other ignorant tyrant."

Emily watched Pickford Marsh process his next words carefully. She could tell she had touched a nerve. He wasn't used to others insulting his abilities nor his acumen. Pickford slowly rubbed his forehead and then looked at her with eyes that reminded her of a lion preparing to eat its young.

"You are just like your mother, proud and strong. She fought me at first too, but eventually relented when she saw the uselessness of resisting the inevitable. I so enjoyed ravishing her. Feeling her body struggle beneath mine. I came close to slitting her throat afterwards, but I was curious to see what our offspring might produce. You are as vile and as manipulative as I am, but that's to be expected. Don't you see? You are the fruit of my loins, Emily. You are my daughter."

Pickford's words suffocated and consumed her like a fire eating up oxygen, leaving nothing but a black residue that marked her soul. She gasped for air, wanting nothing more than to escape his steely gaze and bullwhip tongue. It couldn't be true, but deep inside of her, Emily knew he spoke the truth. The clues had always been there. Her mother had tried to tell her, but the shame was too great.

Pickford circled Emily slowly, looking for any visible signs of weakness. Her stoic silence betrayed little, but he knew she was trying to process the unimaginable truth. The revelation was exhilarating for Pickford causing immense excitement within him. Blood was in the water; the chum had been stirred up. Time to take a bite. Pickford bent down and pressed his lips against Emily's ear.

"That's right," he whispered. "I'm your father, Emily. I'm the anonymous benefactor who paid for your college and fronted the seed money to establish your little magazine. I'm the one who drove Darby Weeks away from you. I'm the one who slipped you countless pieces of information about crooked politicians and adulteress moralists. And I'm the one who is going to snuff out the Stickney bloodline once and for all by taking your love's pathetic little life while you helplessly watch. Imagine the look on poor Darby's face when he realizes who you really are. He will go to his grave questioning everything he has believed as the final drops of blood drain from his body. Darby Weeks will finally realize that he has been betrayed yet again by you, the daughter of Pickford Marsh. Oh! The thought of it gives me shivers of joy!"

"You'll never get away with it!" she yelled.

Pickford snapped his fingers and a muscular woman entered the room, then sat down opposite of his captive guest. The woman's face lacked any warmth or sympathy for Emily's predicament. The executioner eyed her from head to toe making invisible cuts with her eyes.

"My name is Giselle. Your life, as you know it, is over. You belong to me now and I will choose whether you live or die. Do as I say and you might survive unharmed. Fight me and I will personally peel the flesh away from your bones and eat the raw marrow inside. Do you understand me?"

Emily looked at the woman with silent contempt as hot rage slowly built inside of her. Nobody ever got away with threatening her. If Giselle wanted a fight, she would get an epic throw-down from her.

"Answer me," Giselle commanded.

Unclenching her teeth, Emily licked her lips and uttered in defiance, "That shade of bitch looks bad on you."

The pain that overcame Emily next was unbearable. Darkness closed in around her eyes as she struggled to breathe. She heard herself cry out, begging for the end of this torture, but it instead grew to an unimaginable intensity. She yelled for a god she didn't believe in to help her. She even evoked the name of Saint Jude, but it was no use. She was alone in a den of lions with nothing to accompany her but her fear.

Pickford roared with approval as Emily screamed out in pain again and again.

"To suffer and endure great hardship is to be Russian, Emily Baines. Welcome to the family," Pickford cackled before downing a shot of his cherished Kalashnikov vodka. "*Spokoynoy nochi*, my dear, a peaceful night to you!"

***

Looking in through the basement window wells, Finnegan Doyle watched in horror the ongoing brutality being inflicted on Emily. He cringed, remembering the beatings he had endured as a child. The images came crashing back to him: of his mother cowering with fear in the corner of her bedroom as his father repeatedly hit her until her face was so swollen. As Emily continued to suffer, Finn could hardly contain the rage building inside of him.

He wanted to smash through the windows into the underground chamber to rescue her, but he knew it would be fatal to both Emily and himself. Instead, Finn summoned all of his strength and left the remote compound to seek help from the only place and person he knew could stop the monster known as Pickford Marsh. He prayed he wouldn't be too late.

Setting off toward the warm glow of the hotel shimmering in the darkness to the west, Finn labored through knee-high snow, cursing himself for not bringing his snowshoes. With each step, he broke through a thin layer of surface ice before sinking into the soft snow that lay underneath it. His progress was painfully slow as his legs began to numb, but he keep pressing on knowing Emily's life depended on it.

As Finn continued to trudge through the snow-covered fields, he thought through his plan of action. He would wake Darby first. Darby's history with Emily would ensure he'd have the level of concern for her required to help Finn save her. Darby would have to convince Quinn that Emily was in trouble and needed their help. Quinn would then call in his resources and assistance would be on the way. That is, assuming Quinn didn't just arrest Finn on the spot. He would have to be quick.

***

The smell of dank evergreen pierced my nostrils as an invisible hand laced with pine pitch covered my mouth.

"Don't say a flipin' word," a voice commanded as a flashlight began to illuminate the darkness in my bedroom. The hand slowly removed itself from my mouth as my mind cleared. I started to regain my bearings. Glancing at the clock, my brain began to register the early hour. My eyes focused in on the serious face of Finnegan.

"What the hell are you doing here? Haven't you ever heard of using a phone?"

"Phones are never quite secure, Darbs. You know that. Besides, I'm starting to like scaring the bejesus out of you. I need you to come with me now," he said, becoming serious. "Get dressed, we're going for a walk."

"Like hell I am! I'm not going anywhere with you at this time of night. Come back after breakfast," I replied angrily, throwing the pillow over my head.

Finn removed the pillow. "It involves Emily," he said. "If you still care for her at all, you need to come with me now. We don't have a lot of time."

The mention of Emily's name sent my brain into an uncontrollable whirlwind. How did I feel about her? It would have been easier to ask me how many stars were in the heavens than to ask me to process my current emotions for Emily.

"Darby, she's in serious trouble. I can't save her myself. I need you and Quinn to help me." He was beginning to shake.

"So go ask Quinn yourself. He's the head of hotel security. I don't have the power to do anything around here."

"Quinn thinks I'm the cause of all the trouble around here. He'd just assume turn me over to the county sheriff than believe a word I have to say, let alone help me. I need you to persuade him to listen to me for Emily's sake."

"What exactly is the matter with Emily?" I asked.

"Pickford has her, Darby. I saw him hurting her."

"You're mistaken. Emily's in New York, not here."

"No, she never made it back to New York. Pickford took her."

"And how do you know that?" I asked.

184

"I saw her with my own eyes, Darby. She must have been kidnapped by him."

"Why in the world would Pickford kidnap Emily? He doesn't even know her."

"It doesn't matter why, it only matters that he has her now and he is torturing her as we waste time chitchatting."

Hearing the word *torture* ratcheted up my level of concern exponentially. If Emily really was in trouble, I had no choice but to help in any way I could despite my own feelings of inadequacy.

"Tell me exactly what you saw," I said.

Finn recounted what he had witnessed, and I was dressed and walking out the door before he had even finished describing the atrocious scene in detail. We were knocking on Quinn's door two minutes later.

Quinn groggily answered the door. Taking one look at Finn, he reached out and slammed him to the floor. With his knee firmly planted against Finn lower back, Quinn commanded me to get his handcuffs out of his sports coat.

"Wait a minute," I pleaded, trying to diffuse the situation. "We came here to ask you for your help. You need to take a minute and listen to Finn."

"I don't need to hear any of his lies. He can tell it to the judge."

"Quinn…Emily has been kidnapped by Pickford. Now he's torturing her at his compound. We need your help to save her. Please, give us two minutes," I begged, looking him in the eyes. He stared back at me and let my words register in his brain for a moment.

Standing up, Quinn lifted Finn off the floor. "You've got two minutes to convince me that I should believe anything you have to say. Go."

Shaking the feeling back into his arms, Finn calmly repeated the story he told me in my room minutes earlier. The details sounded even more gory and monstrous the second time around. Quinn listened dispassionately, displaying no emotion while the gruesome details were being revealed. Quinn let out a loud breath after Finn had finished his eyewitness account.

"Do you believe him?" he asked, turning toward me.

"Yes," I said. "I don't think Finn is stupid enough to put himself in jeopardy over a lie."

"Let me make a quick phone call and then we'll leave for the compound."

"There's no plowed roads in," Finn replied. "We'll have to go on foot."

"We've got snowshoes in the valet's storage closet. Head down there, I'll join you in a few minutes after I've called in some favors from my FBI friends."

CHAPTER 16

Pickford looked down at Emily's limp but still breathing body lying on the ground and smiled. She wasn't nearly as tough as she thought she was, then again, he'd never seen anyone last very long when matched up against the wicked imagination of Giselle. She was a visionary, a prophet of pain who demanded fidelity through the letting of blood, and a direct descendent of the White Terror leader Lavr Kornilov. There was no limit to Pickford's power or reach with a subservient resource like Giselle at his beck and call. She was the ultimate nuclear option and he knew she would turn on him in an instant if the Voice in the dark instructed her to end his life. He had no choice but to compile with the plan.

The next steps were carefully orchestrated in precise detail in order to guarantee the complete ascendancy of the Marsh family name and the total destruction of the remaining bloodline of its longtime nemesis, Joseph Stickney. With a nod of Pickford's head, his two most loyal employees, the ones he called his cleaners, lifted Emily off the floor and hauled her up to the garage. Wrapping her tightly in blankets, they secured their human cargo to a motorized sled prepared to plunge into the subzero night. They had to reach their destination and finish the task before daybreak, lurking only hours away.

Pickford watched in awe as Giselle silently gather the bloodied tools of her trade and exited the compound as swiftly as she had come. He didn't know where she would go next, but he knew she would return someday once his usefulness was exhausted. The Voice would see to it and command Giselle to eliminate the risk he presented. He thought of his favorite poet and smirked at the irony coursing through his head.

'Oh, what a tangled web we weave when first we practice to deceive.'

For the first time in his life, Pickford Marsh contemplated his own death. *Even kings are killed in battle*, he thought to himself. What would he leave behind and who would be there to receive it? He pondered the matter for a few minutes before extinguishing the lights and ascending to the garage. Perhaps he could still change the outcome. He had to hurry.

***

The thermometer was just south of zero as we entered the crisp, clear night. The forecasted snow squalls had already blown through, allowing the full moon to reflect off the freshly covered snowfields that illuminated the grim face of Finn. Glancing up, I spotted Orion rising over the horizon while Scorpio fled below.

How many nights had I gazed at the ancient hunter and took solace in his companionship? Thousands perhaps. Tonight it gave me fortitude as I stepped into my snowshoes and began the trek toward my destination looming in the east.

The rhythmic crunch of the new snow beneath our feet was hypnotic. Our breakneck pace reflected the sense of urgency that we all felt. The valley's four-foot snow depth made snowshoes a necessity if we were to quickly cut through the backcountry and reach the bunker lair of Pickford Marsh and rescue Emily. I hoped we weren't too late.

The compound was completely dark when we reached it. No lights were shining and no activity could be seen inside. Finn led us to the basement windows where he had seen Emily sprawled on the floor earlier. There was no movement within.

"Where did they go?" I asked, wondering if Finn had indeed misled us after all.

"There were five of them," Finn replied. "Emily, Pickford, another woman, and the two goons.

"If this is a set-up, I'm shooting you first," Quinn threatened Finn.

"I swear they were all here," Finn said.

The sound of a snowmobile coming to life startled us as it accelerated out of the garage and headed toward the western shoulder of Mount Washington. Running to the opposite side of the compound, I caught sight of the rider speeding away from me. He was wearing a distinctive Russian Ushanka hat.

"That's got to be Pickford!" I shouted. "He's getting away."

Entering the still-open garage, I mounted a second sled and brought it to life. Finn jumped on the back as we made chase of Pickford's sled. The headlights radiating from both of our

189

snowmobiles removed any notion of stealth. We could see Pickford and he could see us in close pursuit. The distance between our two sleds remained constant as he bobbed and weaved through the hotel's snow-covered golf course, heading directly for the Marshfield base station. Didn't he know it was a dead end? The frigid air lashed at my face causing tears that peeled away and froze solid to my cheeks. My nasal passages ached, but I continued the pursuit knowing that Pickford had no way out.

Arriving at the base station of the Cog Railroad, Finn and I watched as the sled in front of us executed a 360-degree turn before darting up the tracks and heading for the summit.

"Bad decision," Finn shouted. "He won't get far."

I knew the risks associated with a haphazard ascent of Mount Washington during the winter, and at night no less. Pickford would either slide off the mountain into a ravine or flash-freeze to death above the tree line as the polar winds assaulted the summit. I gave chase anyway. Emily's life was at stake and we needed to know where he had taken her. Finn's tightening grip around my waist informed me that he was not sure about my plan. For all I cared, he could jump off anytime he saw fit.

Continuing our climb, we passed the railway's antiquated water tower falling further behind Pickford's sled as the path grew icier and the slope grew greater. Ten-foot long icicles hung off the water tower threatening to impale us as we sped by, seemingly oblivious to the dangers lurking around us. Our visibility began to blur as another snow squall blew in while a haunting ice fog socked in the summit that loomed above us.

Within minutes, Pickford reached the steep incline known as Jacob's Ladder. The thirty-foot high trestle pitched upward at almost a forty-degree angle. In perfect weather, the journey up it was enough to cause even the bravest of souls to get white knuckles. Tonight it was encased in blue ice six inches thick. A freezing fog shrouded the entire upper mountainside. There would be no escape, but to my amazement Pickford's sled continued to climb the tracks until it disappeared into the whiteout above.

"Where in the world does he think he's going?" Finn shouted. "Hell's in the other direction."

"Get off the sled. I'm going to follow him," I yelled back.

"Do you have a death wish? Don't do it. It's suicide," Finn answered.

"I have no choice, Finn. I have to go."

"He's not going anywhere, Darby. We'll catch him later if the lunatic doesn't plunge to his death."

"Emily probably doesn't have much time, if any," I reminded him. "I have to go after Pickford."

Catching Finn by surprise, I pushed him off the sled and careened up the trestle in pursuit of my family's nemesis. It was like navigating through a wet cotton ball. The whiteout conditions were extreme, made only worse by the ice. Feeling my sled slip beneath me, I realized that there would be no stopping now unless I wanted to slide backwards and plunge to my death.

The engine revved as the sled's skis chattered on the rough ice beneath me. Peering into the fog ahead, I saw nothing as my headlight illuminated a wall of white, and then faintly I saw it: a dark shadow in the distance that grew larger by the second. At first, I thought I was gaining ground on Pickford's sled, but then I realized that the distance between us was closing too fast. His sled tumbled backwards and rammed into mine with such force that I flipped forward over the handlebars and landed with a *thud* on the ice-encrusted track.

The machines careened off the wooden trestle and plummeted into the void below. My body's momentum slowed and then eventually reversed as I began to slide back down the slope. Unable to catch my breath, I clawed frantically at the ice, trying to slow my descent. I crashed into a dislodged ski and felt myself go over the edge as a hand reached out and grabbed a hold off my parka. I dangled above the precipice, looking down into nothing. Craning my neck, I looked over my shoulder at Finn straining to pull me back up onto the track.

"Jesus, Darbs, could you maybe lose a little weight?" Finn said through gritted teeth.

I swayed back and forth, hanging above the hidden ravine below me, unable to say anything at first. After regaining my breath, I told him, "Use two hands."

"Can't do that," Finn groaned. "The ice ax in my other hand is keeping us both from going over."

Removing my belt, I managed to thread it through the wooden timbers above me and buckled it. I hooked one of my arms through the loop and managed to support myself, relieving Finn of the burden and allowing him to reposition himself to help me up.

"Why did you follow me up the track?" I asked him through heavy breaths as I laid on the track, steadying my nerves.

"You pissed me off when you managed to throw me off the sled so easily. I followed you up here determined to kick your ass."

"Well, thanks for the helping hand," I replied.

"Did Pickford go over?" Finn asked.

"His sled came crashing down into mine, but I didn't see him slide over the edge. I didn't see him at all," I admitted.

"Then let's take a closer look," Finn suggested, handed me a pair of crampons and pointing up the track.

We walked with caution up the steep incline looking for any sign or clue as to what had become of Pickford. Unable to see but a few feet ahead, we found nothing until we reached the head of Jacob's Ladder. There in the snow were footprints parallel to the track that continued upward into the whiteout of the summit.

"He's heading for the observatory," I said. "He'll likely seek shelter there."

"Maybe not. The weather station staff maintains a couple of Sno-Cats. They use them to transport and swap out the weekly summit crews. Pickford might be able to commandeer one."

"And go where?" I asked. "He can't see an arm's length in front of him."

"Pickford's scared and we have him on the run. He's trying to escape and live to fight another day. He's smart enough to know a moving target would be harder for us to catch."

I pondered this for a minute while thinking through the events of the last few hours. "No, I think Pickford is intentionally trying to reach the summit. He left his compound heading in this direction before he knew we were there. He also had an opportunity to try to lose us on the open snowfields, but he didn't. He chose to corner himself and climb the cog tracks."

"Maybe he panicked?" Finn suggested.

"A man like Pickford doesn't panic. He always has a deliberate plan."

Finn nodded his head in agreement. "Then let's get to the summit as fast as we can and discover what that plan is. We need to find Emily and make sure she's all right. Only Pickford knows where she is now."

Our pace quickened as our eyes followed the footprints in the snow and for the first time we noticed something else – blood. Drops of blood streaked the snow at our feet. Pickford was alive, and he was hurt. I stopped, glancing up toward the weather observatory. The blowing snow stung my face. The glow of the floodlights on the Sherman Adams building illuminated the fog all around it, serving as a homing beacon and guiding us to our destination.

I looked at Finn. His eyes were wild like a hound in pursuit of a fox. "We have him on the run," he yelled again.

"He's not running from us. He's running towards something he seeks," I observed.

Pickford's plummeting sled was intended to kill me. I was already dead and gone in his mind. He was now focused on something else: the original reason he left his compound earlier in such a hurry. What Pickford was seeking was somewhere up here in the thin air of New England's highest peak. I knew he was determined to succeed at all costs and that was what made him so dangerous.

The stinging wind and plummeting temperatures made the summit a death zone. Upon reaching it, I knew we needed to get inside without delay or we would succumb in a matter of minutes. The gale force winds had erased the footprints we had been following, but it was easy to deduce that Pickford had entered the Sherman Adams building. Banging repeatedly on the outer door of the weather observatory, we were eventually greeted by a befuddled meteorologist.

"Jesus! Where did you two come from?" the staff member on duty, a young meteorologist, shouted as he hauled open the door and pulled us inside. "You know it's minus thirty-eight outside with the wind chill?"

"Tell me something I don't know," I mumbled between chattering teeth.

"Did you let anyone else in?" Finn barked.

"It's four o'clock in the morning," the scientist replied. "Exactly who do you think would be visiting us?"

"There was a snowmobile accident down by Jacob's Ladder. A man fled up here towards the summit. We were following him," I explained.

"He's got to be here. Where is he?" Finn demanded in a hoarse voice.

"Me and another weather observer are the only two people up here. We came up together on Wednesday."

"Where's your partner now?" I asked.

"Still sleeping…he's got the morning shift. Just Marty and I are awake now."

"Marty? You just told us there were only two of you up here," I countered, growing suspicious.

"Marty's the cat." He pointed to the black pile of fur rubbing against my leg. "He's the observatory's mascot and the only full-time resident on top of the *Rockpile*. He's got free reign all over this massive facility in the winter."

"Is it possible that someone could get inside here without you noticing?" Finn questioned.

"No way. The entire building's closed and shuttered for the winter. It's also encased in twenty-eight inches of rime ice. There are only two doors we keep free of the snow and ice. No one can get in here unless we let them in."

"Can we speak to your partner?" I asked. "Maybe he let somebody in without you knowing it?"

"Impossible. We have webcams set up on all the doors and several other cameras pointing out in different directions. I'd see anyone coming or going and I haven't seen anything alive out here for days."

"Can we review your camera feeds to see if the man came this way?" I asked.

"Exactly who are you two?" the baby-faced scientist asked.

"This here is Finnegan Doyle and my name's Darby. Who are you?"

"I'm Jared."

"Well, Jared, a friend of ours is in trouble and her life's in grave danger. We need to find the man we were following since he is the only one who knows where we can find her," I explained. "Will you help us?"

The young meteorologist glanced back and forth between Finn and I trying to decide if he believed our story or not. "I'll get you two some coffee while you review the feeds," he said, deciding to trust us.

"Thanks," Finn said. "And check on your partner. I want to make sure he's where you think he is right now."

Finn and I sat in the office of the observatory's weather room and savored the warmth and smell of the coffee in our hands. Our young savior had shown us how to rewind the digital video steaming from the webcams before leaving us to check on his day-shift partner. Hovering over the computer monitors, we strained our eyes looking for the figure of Pickford Marsh in each of the camera's fields of view. We saw nothing in the main

196

door's webcam feed except our own arrival and had moved on to examining the secondary door's video.

"I don't understand it," Finn said while continuing to scan the video. "We were only like ten minutes behind him, tops. Where the hell is he hiding?"

"I'm not sure he's hiding," I said, thinking through my earlier analysis. "Pickford has to think we're dead and by all rights we should be. In his mind, no one is following him and no one knows he's here."

"So why is he here?" Finn asked. "And why come all the way up here in the middle of the night in bad weather?"

"I don't know," I admitted, "but it had to be urgent."

"Maybe the tapes will tell us something?" Finn said with hope.

Marty the cat rubbed against my leg as we continued to review the webcam feeds, pausing and zooming in at times with no sign of our quarry anywhere. We were wasting precious time we didn't have. Where the hell was Pickford? If he didn't come inside, he'd be dead by now.

"Jared's been gone quite a while," Finn noted. "I don't like it. Something doesn't feel right, Darby"

"We'll give him a few more minutes and then we'll go check on him. He probably just stopped to—"

"Darbs, look down at the cat!" Finn yelled, interrupting me.

Glancing down I caught sight of Marty weaving in and out between my legs. With each tiny step he took, a bloody paw print dotted the steel gray floor.

"Shit, Pickford's already somewhere inside the building!" I stood up, knocking over my chair. Looking back up towards the monitor, a shadowy figure loomed large in a webcam feed, prying off a shutter and climbing in through a remote window of the building.

"Where the hell's the weather guy?" Finn said in a panic. "We need to get to that part of the building now."

Finn's words echoed in the weather room as the lights suddenly flickered and went out, leaving us alone in the darkness of the room. The sound of the purring cat and the blowing wind outside was all I could hear as I fumbled for a flashlight.

"Five bucks says that's not related to the weather," I said.

"With our luck it's the Presence," Finn replied.

"The what?" I asked while illuminating a battery-powered lantern I had found on the shelf next to me.

"You've never heard of the Presence?" Finn continued, bathed in the eerie glow of the light now filling the room. "It's a ghost that walks the summit at night, messing with things and making noise."

"I don't have time for ghost stories, Finn."

"It's not a story," he continued. "Many people have died up here on the old 'Rockpile.' They say their restless spirits inhabit this building."

"He's right," Jared said as he entered the room in a hurry.

"Where the hell have you been?" I asked, shaking off the scare he'd just given me.

"I went to check on Andy, my shift partner. He wasn't in his bunk and the bed was ice cold. He hasn't been there for quite a while, hours if I had to guess."

"When's the last time you saw him?" Finn asked.

"I started my shift at five o'clock last night. We normally work twelve-hour shifts, but Andy stayed with me for a little while before heading back down to the bunkroom. When I didn't find him sleeping there, I went looking for him. He's not in the observatory."

"What about the lights?" I asked.

"The observatory's powered off the electrical grid which reaches us through a cable running alongside the Cog Railroad. We don't usually lose power, but in case we do we have two large kerosene generators in the machine room that can be manually started."

"Why don't you get down there and see if you can get them started," I told Jared. "Finn and I are going to search the other areas of building. The individual we are looking for is already inside the facility somewhere."

"How do know that? Did you find something on the webcam feeds?" Jared replied.

"Yeah…there was a blurred image of a figure climbing in through a window in one of the closed off areas of the building. Also your cat stepped in somebody's blood," I said, setting the lantern down on the floor.

"Oh my God. Whose blood is it?" Jared asked.

"It's either our guy's or Andy's. Now go get the generators started. We need light. When you're done, meet up with us on the main floor of the facilities down by the museum."

"Will do," he said, still looking down at the blood.

"And one more thing," I said. "Be careful, Jared. The man we're seeking has killed before and he won't hesitate to kill you either."

Jared nodded his head before disappearing back into the darkness.

"You trust him?" Finn asked.

"He's just a kid fresh out of college. We've got no choice but to trust him. Now grab that other lantern and let's get going.

If I'm going to run into the Presence up here, I want to see it coming a mile away."

"Good luck with that. Ghosts are invisible," Finn reminded me.

"Only the ones in our imagination," I replied. "True ghosts are really unfinished business that cause us to haunt ourselves."

"Then let's finish this business now and catch the bastard tonight."

If only it was that easy, I thought to myself as we headed out of the room and began our search of the massive Sherman Adams building.

***

"Why are you here?" demanded the Voice. "I did not send for you."

Pickford looked into the darkness toward the direction that the sound had come from, but he saw nothing. "We need to talk, now."

"No, you need to follow directions. All is going as planned, but you have put both of us at risk by coming here."

"There's no risk. Nobody knows I'm here," Pickford answered.

"You fool, the heir is still alive. He's here now searching for you as we speak," the Voice hissed.

"Impossible! I killed him myself. He's at the bottom of Jacob's Ladder," Pickford said smugly.

"Your arrogance disgusts me. If the heir doesn't kill you tonight, I will do it myself. You're no longer an asset to me. Good riddance, Iscariot. "

"Wait…I need to discuss our deal…Hello? Answer me damn it!"

The Voice was gone, replaced by the drone of the wind outside and sounds of approaching footsteps echoing down the hall.

***

"Damn, it's cold in here," Finn observed.

"Only the weather observatory is inhabited in the winter. There's no heat, water, or electricity in this part of the building. They shut it all down," I said as we walked past the building's gift shop. "You want me to buy you some Mount Washington ear muffs?"

Finn ignored my comment. His attention was drawn to the outer windows of the long curved hallway. They were glazed with ice and snow and backlight by the emergency powered floodlights. The windows seemed to move in the blowing wind like an alien life form awakening from a long winter's sleep.

"They're absolutely beautiful," he said, mesmerized by the abstract curves and bends.

"The summit crews affectionately call them ice fossils," Jared's voice called from behind us as he walked down the hallway and rejoined us outside the gift shop.

"What's the status on the generators?" I asked.

"I can't get them started. To tell you the truth, I'm not really that mechanical. I need some help."

"I'll go with him," Finn volunteered. "I can fix anything."

"Okay, I'll keep searching this level," I replied. "Get the lights and heat on as soon as you can."

"If you find him, Darby, don't kill him. I want a crack at interrogating Pickford," he said with a demonic smile before darting back down the hallway with Jared.

Don't kill him? For the first time, I thought about what I would do if I actually found Pickford hiding in the labyrinth of the summit building. The idea of hurting him or any other person never crossed my mind. Even though I was a decorated veteran, I didn't think I could ever make myself kill again. I shined the light down the hallway in front of me and thought about creating an excuse to retreat to the generator room to help Finn and Jared restore the power. *This is no time for fear*, I told myself. *Emily needs you.*

A sudden sound emanating from the observatory's weather museum up ahead refocused my attention to the task at hand. Creeping along the hallway, I entered the summit's museum in a crouch, scanning the area in front of me with my lantern. Glancing up, I took in several informative displays dedicated to the extreme weather and unique geology that made up the summit of Mount Washington. But it was a black and photo that caught my eye. A mythical catamount sat perched next to a tall mountain cairn. *Follow the catamount,* I repeated under my breath. Rounding the corner, my light illuminated the towering figure of Pickford Marsh leaning against an outer window.

"Why are you following me?" he said without any emotion or surprise that I was there.

"I want to know what you've done with Emily," I replied with less composure.

"What makes you think I've done anything with her?"

"Finn said he saw you torturing her in the basement of your compound tonight."

Pickford let out a hideous laugh that reverberated in the open space of the museum. "Why would you believe anything that boy says? He's a terrorist whose sole focus is to destroy my company's operations. He'd say anything to get you to help him."

"Then why did you flee your compound when we arrived?"

"What are you talking about? I didn't even know you were there. I received word through a very reliable source that Finnegan Dole was planning on destroying the communication towers on top of the summit tonight. My company owns these towers and I came here in an effort to stop him."

"You lie," I said with growing anger. "You and I are going to take a little walk and get things sorted out with Finn."

"I'm not going anywhere with you and I most certainly won't get within ten feet of that lunatic Finnegan Doyle."

"You're too late for that, Finn's just down the hall," I lied.

Pickford looked past my shoulder, his face betraying a hint of fear.

"Tell me where Emily is and I'll keep Finn away from you," I said. "I know she was with you tonight."

"Yes," he conceded, "she did visit me tonight, but that is none of your concern."

"I swear to God if you've hurt her—"

"Why would I hurt my own daughter?" Pickford said, cutting me off.

The words hit me like a Russian AK round. Stunned, I just stood there in shock not knowing what to say.

"You didn't know?" Pickford asked, looking deep into my eyes. "Oh how precious." He laughed. "The love of your life never told you she was a Marsh." His laughter grew louder, penetrating the dark silence as I deflated like a day-old balloon.

"I don't believe a thing you say. She's not your daughter." I was shaking my head in disbelief.

"Search your heart, Darby," Pickford said wickedly. "Doesn't it all makes sense now? The reason she left you so many times? She knew that if you ever discovered the truth about her, you would never recover."

A wave of dizziness swept over me as my eyes lost focus. It couldn't be true. Emily could not be Pickford's daughter. She couldn't have kept that secret from me.

"Sorry, I didn't mean to spill the beans on our family secret," Pickford hissed, "but I do intend to spill the last of your family's blood," he roared as he withdrew a pistol and cocked the hammer back. "I killed your father and your grandfather and now Emily has helped me to kill you. Goodbye, Darby…Stickey…Weeks."

The sound of gunfire was deafening as I collapsed onto the wooden floor. Shards of broken glass rained down on me as a wave of arctic air flowed into the museum, chilling my body. I laid there waiting for the pain to strike, but it never came. Peeking up through one of my half opened eyes, I spied Finn in the faint glow of my lantern holding a still-smoking forty-five-caliber pistol. Pickford was gone.

"Are you all right, Darby?" Finn asked.

I checked my body before answering. "Yeah, I think I'm fine," I said, hardly believing it myself. "What happen to Pickford?" I asked through a dry quivering mouth.

"I just shot and killed him…blew him right out the window," he said, moving closer to me. Finn stopped at the breached window and looked out through the shattered pane of glass.

I rose to my feet. "So much for him telling us where Emily is."

"You're welcome, by the way," Finn replied. "This makes us even now. I've repaid the debt. I don't owe you anything."

I nodded my head, understanding his words. "Emily's gone isn't she?" I asked.

Finn shrugged his shoulders. "You heard him. He wouldn't hurt his own daughter."

"He was lying, Finn…playing with my mind."

"If you say so," he replied as the lights flickered back to life and the radiator pipes began to clank. "You better call Quinn and tell him what happened."

"Maybe he found Emily," I said, wishing it were true.

"Make the call, Darby," Finn repeated. "Our work here is done."

CHAPTER 17

Quinn Matthews and a slew of FBI agents arrived at the summit with the rising sun of the new day. The winds had finally receded, dying down after a long night of assaulting the peak. A fresh six inches of snow had reshaped the evening's violent landscape, making it look fresh and pristine like a tranquil white sand beach while the skies above surrounded us in a vast ocean of deep blue, an ocean that threatened to pull me under.

"We believe Emily might still be alive," Quinn announced knowing the first question that I would ask. "The FBI took into custody two men on snowmobiles returning to the Marsh compound. They are being interrogated as we speak. They aren't cooperating, but once they learn that their boss has been killed I expect they'll change their tune."

I nodded my head and exhaled, releasing a mass of tension that had clung to me throughout the night. This nightmare was finally coming to an end.

"The body outside is gone," Quinn announced.

"I'm glad you got it stowed away," I replied, finally finding my voice. "I don't want to see his lifeless body."

"No, you don't understand. Pickford's body is gone. It's missing," Quinn clarified.

"What do you mean it's missing?" Finn asked in disbelief. "Darby and I both saw him sprawled out in the snow below the museum's window. I shot him myself."

"His body's not there," Quinn repeated. "The agents and I just left the scene. There's a pool of frozen blood, but no body."

"Could he have survived and crawled away?" I asked.

"I shot him three times point blank with a forty-five…he tumbled and fell fifteen feet from out the window. Nobody could survive that," Finn said.

"I agree," Quinn declared. "Given how much blood we found below the window and how cold it was outside last night, I'd say Pickford Marsh is definitely dead."

"Then how does a body just disappear?" I asked.

"I'm thinking it was dragged away by someone or something," Quinn theorized.

"What do you mean by 'something'?" Finn asked.

"The new snow and high winds last night erased any surface evidence that might have existed, but I did find a partial print on the leeward side of the building," Quinn revealed.

"What kind of print?" I asked.

"Animal…it looks to be a cat of some kind."

Finn and I looked at each other thinking the same thing, but knowing it was impossible.

"The National Guard is currently sweeping the summit area with two Blackhawk helicopters. They're looking for the body or anything unusual. If the body's out there, they'll find it," he said with confidence.

"What about Jared and the missing weather observer? Could they have moved the body?" I asked, thinking through the possibilities.

"They found the missing crew member's body in the cold storage room just below the instrument deck. His neck was broken."

"Murdered?" Finn asked.

"It appears the guy fell as he was returning from chipping away the rime ice from the weather instruments. It was most likely an accident. The agents are interviewing Jared now, but his actions aren't consistent with those of a murderer."

"Yeah, plus he was with us most of time," I reminded Finn. "He didn't have a motive to kill his partner, nor would he have had enough time to move Pickford's body afterward."

"I think we should just let the investigators do their job. It's been a hell of a night. In the meantime, there's a Sno-Cat waiting to take you two back down the mountain. As soon as I hear anything regarding Emily, I will let you know," Quinn assured me.

"Are there agents looking for her?" I asked.

"Yes, there's a massive search party looking for her. They're scouring the Crawford Notch area, but they haven't found anything yet."

"Have they checked around Thoreau Falls?" Finn asked.

"They will," Quinn said, "but there's a lot of caves and crevices to check."

"The Pit of Hell and Well of Lost Souls," I said.

***

Elsie Fitzgerald stood outside the AMC hut at the edge of the Lakes of the Clouds, throwing chunks of freshly butchered meat into the snow. The animal watched her from a distance, instinctively knowing the dangers that humans presented. It circled closer, enticed by the prospect of an easy meal. Sniffing the air, the beast snapped at a piece of flesh all the while keeping a watchful eye on Elsie.

"Come now, Sasha. You know me, old friend," Elsie said with a laugh. "Eat up girl, you need the energy after last night's storm."

The beast snarled at Elsie as she inched closer to the great cat, rattling the core of her body. Elsie had been feeding the cats and closely guarding the knowledge of their existence for many years. She had grown to love them like children and respected their awesome power. The cat before her, the one she called Sasha, was the most ornery one of the two mating pairs that stalked the wooded highlands of the North Country. Most days she gave the reclusive cats a wide berth, but today she needed their help. Elsie laughed at the irony. What better way to dispose of a threat to the environment than to have it consumed by the environment?

The great cat's ears perked up just before it vanished into the nearby tree line. A moment later, a helicopter rose up out of the ravine unannounced, startling Elsie as the thump of its rotors echoed off the exposed granite. She waved to the pilot, hoping he would move along and leave her be. Instead the drab olive-colored aircraft set down near the hut, whipping up snow and ice that stung her face. Elsie stepped back as several men exited the helicopter and walked toward her. Their presence annoyed her, but she relented when they told her she'd be coming with them.

Elsie shielded her head as the law enforcement agents took her into custody, ushering her into the protective shelter of the hut.

"What did you do with the body?" the lead FBI agent asked.

"I didn't kill anyone," Elsie shot back.

"Elsie, now is the time to come clean and cooperate," Quinn said, inserting himself into the conversation.

"I already told you, I didn't kill anyone."

"I know that," Quinn responded. "Somebody else shot Pickford Marsh, but you stole and disposed of his body. We want to know why."

"You know nothing," Elsie replied defiantly.

The lead FBI agent retook control of the interrogation.

"We have video of you exiting the summit building early this morning hauling Mr. Marsh's body behind you on a sled. We also just witnessed you feeding what appears to be human flesh to a wild animal. As we speak, agents are collecting samples of that flesh to analyze and compare it to Mr. Marsh's DNA. I am certain that it will be a one hundred percent match. You can cooperate right now, or you can be charged with any number of federal charges and spend the rest of your life in a tiny cell in a federal prison."

Elsie looked back and forth between Quinn and the other agent knowing that she was trapped with no way out. She decided to play the only card she had left.

"Elsie, this is the one chance you have to make things right," Quinn added.

"When I was eleven years old," Elsie began in a quiet voice, "my mother knelt down and kissed me on the cheek one morning as I was heading out the door to school. She looked me in eyes and said, 'Make me proud, Elsie.' It was the last time my mother ever said my name. I would later find out that while I practiced my morning arithmetic at school, my mother was raped, her throat was cut, and she was left to die all alone in the woods. Everyone knew who did it, but the criminal was untouchable since his family controlled half the North Country. My father was incensed. Bound and determined to see justice served, he went to the only other family who could possibly help, but they turned him away. Just shut him out. My father made a pledge that day to make both families suffer as much as he had suffered. Unfortunately he died before he could honor that pledge. Today, half of that justice was served."

The room was silent as each man attempted to reconcile the pain that existed in Elsie's heart with the need to uphold the law.

Quinn broke the silence. "Tell me what you did with the body, Elsie."

Elsie pulled a book off the makeshift library shelves that lined the windowsill of the hut at the Lakes of the Clouds. She opened it and read aloud, *"Towards thee I roll, thou all-destroying but unconquering whale; to the last I grapple with thee; from hell's heart I stab at thee; for hate's sake I spit my last breath at thee."*

Throwing the book on the floor, Elsie looked up at Quinn. "He's in the Pit of Hell and the Well of Lost Souls."

***

211

Sometimes, if we're lucky, our worst nightmares come true. Other times they linger just below the surface, promising to jump out and paralyze us at any moment. We can't predict when it will happen or how our deepest fear will manifest itself in the daylight, but too often the not knowing is worse than the actual occurrence.

Emily awoke from one nightmare only to find herself submerged in a pit of hell awaiting her earthly penance. She'd been here once before, in what now seemed like a lifetime ago. The experience so shocked her that she had willed it out of existence, forcing it back inside where it resided as the blackest of terrors, locked in the deepest corner of her subconscious. Its awakening carved out whatever courage remained within her. She knew that she was now completely alone in the well of lost souls.

The stench was wretched, forcing her to breathe through the elbow of her jacket. Even though filtered through her sleeve, the air still made her gag. The darkness was a weapon as Emily recoiled in fear touching her eyes trying to determine if they were open or closed. She shook, unable to fathom her precarious existence. "Hello?" she cried out, hoping someone would hear her, but the only response that returned was the fading echo of her own voice. She clawed at the filth all around her, trying to find traction amongst the human detritus, but only sunk lower with each failed movement.

The natural cistern, which was cut into the hard granite, had been used for more than half a millennia as a primal dumping ground for the dead. The ancient bone yard festered with vermin who had awoken from their winter sleep to gorge themselves on the recent arrivals. Emily felt them move through her hair, darting in and out of her ears and down the small of her back. She tried to shake them off, but only succeeded in accelerating their movements. Hundreds of legs cascaded over her cold flesh as she clenched her lips praying the pests wouldn't burrow into her mouth and down her throat.

Unable to maintain her sense of calm any longer, Emily thrashed her head from side to side, screaming out for Darby, while regretting all the pain that she had caused him. *Please God, give me another chance. I don't want to die.* Her deep sobs filled the well, reverberating through the chamber and sounding like a dead chorus of wails.

The well of lost souls ached and welcomed its newest member to their forgotten club. As the last of her echoes faded and silence returned to the dark, Emily saw the faintest pinprick of light high above her. *Is this the light that people see at the end when they die?* She asked herself this as she slipped further from the land of the living. Resigned to her fate, Emily summoned all of her remaining strength and lunged upward while yelling out, "Just get it over with!"

"Emily?" a voice called. "Emily, is that you? Please let it be you!"

She felt the weight on her body lessen as layers of decay were removed all around her and hands grabbed hold of her, pulling her up into the light. She couldn't open her eyes, but she could feel the warmth of another living being as it held her and told her she would be all right. She didn't know if she was still alive or dead, but the fear was no longer there.

***

Giselle watched from a distance in silent contempt as the local authorities descended upon the well of lost souls. Both her handler and her employer were now gone, freeing her to go where she yearned to be. Her time in the North Country was over. Giselle would now return to the city of her birth and await the inevitable that was sure to come. One enemy was destroyed while the other had grown stronger with knowledge. The heir would eventually return to the ancient land and seek to regain what was lost. She would be watching and waiting.

Thus I give up the spear, Giselle thought to herself, *at least until we meet again when I will return as the lion and you shall perish in my den by the sea.*

***

"We found her!" yelled a first responder who emerged from the sliver of a crevice cut into the cliff face. "She looks like hell, but she's alive."

"We never would have found her if it wasn't for you Finn," I said, bursting with emotion.

"Without the riddles and the picture on the window, I wouldn't have known what I was looking for," he said modestly. "I'm just glad she's alive."

We stood at the top of the drop-off near Thoreau Falls and watched in silence as the emergency crews lowered Emily down the cliff face and onto a waiting ATV. She was carted off to a nearby clearing before being transported by DHART, to the intensive care unit at Dartmouth Hitchcock Medical Center. Emily would have a long recovery ahead of her—both physically and emotionally—but she would live.

"You won't believe what's inside that hellhole," said Quinn, rejoining us after being briefed by his FBI friends. "There are hundreds upon hundreds of human remains inside the well with thousands of cicadas crawling around. We might have stumbled upon the final resting place of all those missing women."

"It might finally prove what has only been a rumor for the past hundred years: the Marsh family's fetish for young women and their untimely disappearances," I said with remorse.

"The state forensics unit is going to be busy for a long time trying to identify who's in there. However, they've already positively identify two victims," Quinn added.

"Who?" I asked in a daze.

"Jacques Robarge, or at least what's left of him."

"And the other?" Finn inquired.

"It seems the missing body of Pickford Marsh has been found."

"How in the hell did he get from the summit to here?" I pondered.

"By the *all-destroying but unconquering enemy*," Quinn replied.

"What?" I asked.

"It's not important," Quinn said.

"The only way his body could have been moved so quickly is if someone else was on top of the summit with us last night," I deduced, thinking through the possibilities. I looked at Quinn, but he offered me no opinions.

"This is an FBI investigation now," Quinn said. "They'll be thorough and they won't rest until every unanswered question has been answered. Let's let them do their jobs."

"Thank you, Quinn, for all your help," I said thinking of Emily.

"And thank you for not arresting me last night," Finn said through half a smile.

"I'm sure I'll get another chance," Quinn said half joking while looking Finn directly in the eyes.

"Until me meet again," Finn said with a laugh.

"You can count on it," Quinn shot back.

215

The DHART helicopter buzzed low over our heads on its way to the hospital in Lebanon, New Hampshire. I couldn't help but wonder about Emily. I wished I could have seen her and told her myself that she was going to be OK. I knew I loved her, but a part of me wondered how the two of us could ever be together – for she was a Marsh and I was a Stickney. Shakespeare's own words rattled in my head. *My only love sprung from my only hate.* If there was no happy ending in his love story, how could there ever be one in mine?

CHAPTER 18

"My life's been nothing but a complete lie," Emily confessed as Father Callaghan leaned over the hospital bed and adjusted her pillow. "Even my birth was marred."

"You think my life's been an easier?" Father Callaghan responded without the faintest trace of sympathy. Emily laughed at Callaghan's complete lack of bedside manner. She should have known better than to show any self-pity to him.

"Do you know what it's like to hate, Father?" Emily asked, feeling numb inside.

"More than you know, young lady."

"Aren't priests suppose to be benevolent?" she pressed.

Father Callaghan stared into Emily's eyes, seeing the same fear and confusion that had troubled him a half a century ago in the killing fields of Vietnam. He knew all too well the sense of helplessness and anger that coursed through her veins. He had never wanted to talk about his own feelings, preferring to self-medicate his demons with drams of scotch and bourbon. Today, he decided to give words to those fears knowing that both Emily and he needed to hear them.

"I first became acquainted with hate in Vietnam," Callaghan began in his gruff voice, "but I didn't fully experience that emotion until 9/11. At Ground Zero, I offered sacraments to the dead and encouragement to the living. For two hundred and sixty straight days, we dug in the dirt, unearthing almost twenty thousand human remains. Every day was an open wound and every night was an Irish wake. We pulled two hundred and ninety-three intact bodies from the scorched earth. Venom poisoned my heart, straining my relationship with God."

"How did you get past it?" Emily whispered.

"I found salvation among the Lakota Sioux," he replied with a heavy sigh. "I ran away from New York, attempting to lose myself amongst the Black Hills. The voice of God spoke through the tribal elders. They recounted the death of General Custer and their own misery. Through their example, I learned how to forgive, but never forget."

"I thought I was going to die all alone in that pit," Emily said. "I thought I'd been forgotten. I haven't given anyone much of a reason to remember me."

"There once was an Italian poet named Antonio Porchia," Father Callaghan recounted. "He wrote that, 'one lives in hope of becoming a memory.' How we treat people as we travel through life is a reflection of how we feel about ourselves.

Learn how to love yourself, Emily, and others will find you irresistible."

"I don't know if I can do that," Emily admitted.

"Hm. I never thought I could like a Marsh," Father Callaghan replied. "Miracles really do happen."

***

"Have you ever heard of the Christmas Truce of World War I?" Silas asked after downing a glass of bourbon-infused eggnog.

"I've only heard bits and pieces of the story," I replied while watching the snow begin to fall outside the window. "I always thought it was nothing more than a myth."

"Oh, I guarantee you it was no myth," Silas said, puffing out his chest.

"Please don't tell me you were there. I know you aren't that old."

"No, I wasn't there, but my father, your great grandfather, was. He called it the greatest spontaneous celebration of humanity and brotherhood that the world had ever seen. Tommies and Jerries exchanging gifts, burying their dead, and playing football matches in No Man's Land between hundreds of miles of trenches. For a brief moment, there was peace on Earth and goodwill to men. All was quiet on the Western Front."

"The unknown was know and there was peace," I said, quoting a sermon I remembered from my youth, another Christmas miracle two thousand years later.

"Do you know what is missing from your life, Darby?"

I could name hundreds of things that I thought were missing from my life – my father, my childhood and my innocence, to name a few. However, as the heavy flakes began to fall with more intensity, my view of the outside world became more obscured. A sense of contentment settled over me. I felt safe inside the ramparts of the old hotel like an immortal being walking amongst the living. Nothing could harm me here.

"Nothing's missing," I finally answered. "My life's come full circle and is complete."

"No," Silas grumbled. "She's missing, numb nuts."

"You think the head of Tither Publishing, someone who targets people and then blackmails them, is the positive force that is missing from my life?"

"Love and hate are beasts, but the one you feed is the one that grows."

"I don't need her," I lied.

"We only need three things in life to be happy: someone to love, something to do, and a good beer. By my count, you have only acquired one courtesy of our friend Easton Crow."

"Emily's not the answer to my happiness anymore," I said. "She's changed, Silas."

"As sure as people can change for the worse, they can also change for the better. I always try to remember who people were before circumstance and heartache transformed them. Each of us has an amazing capacity to shape the lives of others. How we choose to use that power is what makes each of us unique."

As much as I liked to dismiss Silas and his ridiculous long-winded harangues, I had to admit that he was actually starting to make sense. In fact, I had begun to realize that most of the things that Silas said had kernels of truth in them.

"So what am I supposed to do?" I asked.

"Seek out the two things missing to make your trinity of happiness complete, my boy! Must I do all the thinking around here? That's the problem with youth today. They lack any common sense. When I was your age…"

I stopped listening and turned my attention to a newly arrived letter from Horatio. Removing the stationary from the envelope, I began to read his finely crafted script.

Dear Darby -

Word has reached me that your quest has been concluded successfully. The truth has been revealed and the damsel in distress has been saved. I congratulate you whole- heartedly on a job well done. Pass on my well wishes to Ms. Baines and my nincompoop brother.

If I know my meddling sibling at all, he has most likely professed to you the three key elements of happiness. I trust that you have come to your senses and have consummated your relationship with Ms. Baines. Assuming this to be true, it would seem that all you are missing in order to be happy is 'something to do.' I am writing in hopes of rectifying this situation.

I have made the decision to retire from my position at Dartmouth College and seek out new adventures in the world. My departure has been sorely overdue. Prior to leaving, I was granted the privilege of naming my own successor. I can think of no better guardian of the stacks than you, Darby. There are endless secrets and intrigue to be found in the special collections. They await a new champion of discovery while I enjoy discovering the White Nights of Peter. Oh, one more thing, you will need the assistance of a shrewd College Archivist to aid in your new literary quests. Somehow, I think you will be able to find someone who has a plethora of informational sources and who is good at digging up dirt.

Warmest Regards,
Horatio B.

"…and by the time I was nine years old I had already retired from my first job. Are you even listening to me, Darby?

You need to find a new career. Stop lollygagging around here like some leaf-peeping tourist feeling sorry for yourself."

"I think I just found a new job," I said.

"And what line of work would that be?" he asked.

"Books and crooks."

"Somehow I think my brother's paw prints are all over this."

"Indeed, Silas. Indeed."

***

Emily entered the attorney's office and took a seat in a high-back, leather-winged chair and wondered why she had come. *Triumph or maybe closure?* She did not want to be here, but knew it was the first step in her long road to recovery.

"Thank you for coming, Ms. Baines," the lawyer began. "I know this must be quite difficult for you."

"Actually, I don't really know why I'm here," Emily replied.

"Maybe I was misinformed," the lawyer continued, "but I was under the impression you already knew that Mr. Marsh was your father."

To hear those words again caused yellow bile to rise up into her throat, leaving the bitterest of tastes in her mouth.

"He wasn't a father in any sense of the word. He was a cruel, wicked man who I hope spends an eternity burning in hell and being tormented by all the souls of those he raped and killed!"

The lawyer shifted in her seat feeling quite uncomfortable, but pressed on knowing this was her last appointment of the day. "I don't know much about Mr. Marsh's personal life, I'm only representing his estate as the executer of his will. This won't take long so let's just get to it, shall we?"

222

Emily nodded, regretting her momentary loss of control. She no longer recognized the person she had become. Her thoughts and emotions were foreign and unrestrained, raw impulses that chipped away at her fragile sense of self. *Who the hell am I anymore?*

"Ms. Baines, you have been named as the sole beneficiary of the Marsh family estate. Mr. Pickford Marsh has left his entire fortune to you. There are no other living blood relatives. You get everything including complete control of the Aqua-Nord Corporation and all its entities. Congratulations Ms. Baines, you are now one of the richest women on the planet."

Emily ignored the woman's words. Her eyes looked past the attorney and she focused her sight on a framed sign hanging ever so crookedly on the wall just above the talking head.

Death leaves a heartache no one can heal,
And love leaves a memory no one can steal.

She laughed at the sentiment. Her heart ached – not for the passing of Pickford Marsh, but for what he took from her. And as for Darby, she would have paid her entire inheritance to any thief capable of pilfering her memories of him. Then a single clear thought materialized in the fog of her brain. For the first time in months, Emily knew what to do.

"Does your firm handle corporate law?" she asked, boiling up with excitement.

"Yes, I have partners that specialize in it. Why do you ask?"

"I have big plans for Aqua-Nord," she said as a smile broke out on her face. "Here's what I want to do."

***

Silas looked up at the hotel's grandfather clock and then checked it against his own pocket watch. Withdrawing an ornate key from his sports coat, Silas inserted it into the face of the antique clock and turned the crank clockwise precisely thirteen times. A look of consternation filled his face as he adjusted the hands of the clock until they displayed the correct time of day. With the task completed, he let out a noticeable sigh and turned to face me.

"What's wrong?" I asked.

"I once had a friend who was always spouting off about human nature and the concept of change. My friend said to me one day, 'Silas, they always say time changes things, but you actually have to change them yourself.' I never fully appreciated the bittersweet truism of this sentiment until this very moment. Did you know that for the past ninety-seven years, a member of our family has opened and closed the summer season of this grand hotel by stopping and starting this grandfather clock? I've had the honor myself for the past fifty-seven years."

Looking at Silas, I saw sincerity on his face and heard a serious tone in his voice. His lucidness sucked me in and made me want to listen to him for the first time in my life.

"This Elliot Clock Company timepiece is over two hundred years old," Silas continued. "My grandfather had it brought over from Europe with him. It is the last remaining connection I have to the old family. Now with my own hand, I have caused its death. The honored tradition ends with me."

"What are you talking about, Silas?"

"Progress! The most vile eight lettered word in the English language. The hotel's winterization is now complete and year-round operation is at hand. This old clock's unique purpose is now obsolete."

"It can still tell us the time," I said, looking at the bright side.

"A mere shimmer of its former glory. It will grow dusty in obscurity." He touched the three wood spires on top of the clock. "Future guests will never know that it was once the warm heartbeat of this hotel. The focal point of all activity during the summer seasons."

"As long as we don't forget, its place in history will never fade," I added after a moment of reflection.

"Then remember for both of us since my days are numbered too. The clock and I are one in the same, Darby. Remove our purpose and we soon fade into the shadows of history."

"If you don't mind me asking, who was this friend of yours that was so concerned with change?"

"His name was Andrej Varhola, but most people just called him Andy. He was an artist of some kind. He used to do a lot of sketching and graphic design up here at the hotel. He gave me a whole mess of his drawings once, but I never really did care for them. Just an overkill of pastel colors, panels and Campbell soup cans. Like they say, if you don't understand what you're looking at, it must be art."

Andrej Varhola? Once again I was flabbergasted by the realization that Silas had crossed paths with yet another giant of history, but he had no realization of its importance. He just walked through life living in the moment without a care in the world. How I so envied him in this moment.

"Sometimes I feel like my purpose in life has already come and gone, Silas. What does it say about someone whose greatest accomplishments at my age are already in the past?"

"It says you're a royal dumbass."

"What?" I said, shocked by his bluntness.

"Anyone who believes that their life is defined by one moment in time is a dumbass. Life is about opportunities and commitments. You prepare yourself for whatever life has in store for you and then seize the opportunities when they arrive, whether you expect them or not."

"How do you prepare for the unexpected?" I asked. "I can't seem to see past the moment at hand let alone any future opportunities."

"You must open yourself up entirely and be unafraid to live without boundaries. Most people fail to see that the walls they build up on a daily basis with their own two hands are really an abode of self-incarceration. They constrain themselves for the fear of the uncertainty of life."

"Unconstraint living is the fastest way to premature death," I pointed out. "Walls protect us and keep us secure from things that are dangerous."

"Ah yes, the Frost edict: 'Good fences make good neighbors,' but they also make for a lousy society. Sheltering yourself from the unsavory or unpleasant is an act of selfishness, Darby. Life is to be experienced. We love, we ache, and we learn in between. That's the beauty of being truly alive."

"Many of the things I want I can't have," I mused.

"The French have always had the unique ability of summing up matters of the heart succinctly. For example, take their phrase *la douleur exquise*. It expresses the feeling of excruciating pain that comes from wanting someone you can't have. Reassess what you want and balance it out against what you truly need. Needs are acquirable, wants are optional."

"I'll think over that pearl of wisdom while I sleep tonight," I said.

"As our friend Melville would say, 'Think not is my eleventh commandment; and sleep when you can is my twelfth.' And with that I shall retire to my own chamber."

"Goodnight, Silas. Sleep well my great uncle."

I watched as Silas made his way toward the elevator. As the door opened, he greeted the lift operator with a shot. "Ernie, what took you so long? I could have died here waiting for you."

The employee was all too familiar with his act and playfully fired back, "Had I known that, I would stopped for a sandwich on the way down." The two continued their verbal sparring as the elevator door closed and the lift ascended to top floor.

I looked back at the antique clock and realized for the first time today that it was Christmas Eve, a night of eternal hope and enduring peace. It was also a moment of deafening silence. The bustle of the hotel had shut down hours ago as a heavy snow continued to fall outside. As Joseph Stickney's two hundred-year-old grandfather clock inched past midnight, I walked the hallways looking for something or someone.

The crackle of the fireplace and the moose head standing sentry above it greeted me as I straddled the threshold of the Parlor, one foot in the present and the other firmly planted in the past. The scent of spiced oranges and fresh cut evergreens filled the air. I hadn't set foot in this room since the funeral. I had avoided it at all costs. However, the room had a history and I owed it one last visit.

Stepping into the room, I glanced up at the mini rotunda ceiling painted with the faintest blue of a midsummer sky. There, I thought about everyone who had come before me and everyone who had died along the way. I ran my fingers over the top of the piano sitting in the middle of the room. I had denounced the instrument shortly after my father died. It once was a source of joy between him and I, but now it was only a voice of sorrow. Sitting down, I lifted the cover off the keys and looked directly into my past. I began to play, and the opening refrain of a nineteenth century Ukrainian carol cried out as my father entered the room.

I always loved it when you played that song, I heard him whisper in my ear.

I continued to play the *Carol of Bells*, refusing to open my eyes as my heart ached and the tears fell.

You know it wasn't your fault. I had to go for your protection. It was my choice.

I appreciated the lie, but kept playing with increasing intensity as he began to walk around the room with his head tilted back and arms stretched out.

Look around you, Darby. This is your family, this is your history, and this is your future. There's nothing left for me to do, but you have a lifetime ahead of you. You can still make a difference, but you need to let go of everything holding you back.

My fingers ached, matching my heart, as I pounded out the closing refrain. My father's words echoed in the dark as the piano's final note rang out. I slammed my fist into the keys as my eyes flew open. My father was gone, but I had just arrived.

"You play as well if not better than your father," another voice called out.

Raising my head, I spied Georgina Sinclair leaning against one of the rotunda's support columns in the room.

"I didn't know you knew my father," I replied, regaining my composure.

Georgina moved closer and took a seat next to me on the piano bench.

"Not too many people know this," she said with a grin on her face, "but I started at this hotel as a cocktail waitress. I watched your father entertain guests on this very same piano every night. He was an amazing musician."

"I miss him," I said with a sigh. "This might sound crazy, but I heard him talking to me while I was playing just now."

"You're not crazy, Darby. Lots of people have claimed to see ghosts in our hotel. Your great grandmother, Princess Carolyn, is said to routinely walk these hallways in the wee hours of the morning, checking to make sure all of her guests are happy and safe. I keep telling her that's my job." Georgina laughed.

"I'm surprised you stayed all these years," I said. "I don't understand why so many people chose to remain here…Quinn, Flavio, and you."

"We have all stayed because of your family. Your grandfather was very loyal to his employees. He mentored and promoted those with potential. He even believed that an awkward cocktail waitress could someday run all this," she said, spreading her arms out and looking up into the rotunda.

I watched as Georgina mouthed the words *thank you* up into the heavens as the lights flickered in reply. "Did you just see that?" I asked in disbelief.

"I already told you, everyone thinks this place is special. Even the ghosts refuse to leave."

CHAPTER 19

The elevator door opened announcing my arrival at the 44th floor of Tither Publishing's global headquarters. I stood motionless inside the lift trying to decide if I should exit into the nerve center of hypocrisy or slink back into the chaos of the Saint Patrick's festivities flowing through the streets of New York. I caught the receptionist studying me with an eye of bemusement wondering why I hadn't exited immediately onto the floor. Many gudgeons had visited Tither in the past hoping to exact revenge for exposing their sins to the world. The guards flanking the foyer of the elevator were prepared for any trouble I might offer. Flashing my visitor's pass, I exited the lift and parked myself in front of the receptionist's desk.

"Can I help you?" she asked in a suspicious tone.

"My name is Darby Weeks and I'd like to see Ms. Emily Baines," I replied with a dry throat.

"Do you have an appointment?" The receptionist sighed, already guessing my answer.

"No, but if you could just tell her I'm here, I'm sure she would see me."

"Sir, the President of Tither Publishing doesn't meet with anyone without an appointment and if I want to keep my job, I don't 'just tell her' someone is here. Do you understand that?"

"Yes, ma'am," I said, nodding my head. "If it wouldn't be too much trouble then, could you give this to Ms. Baines for me?" I placed the Medal of Honor on the counter. "I really don't have any use for it and considering what she's been though recently, I think she deserves it a lot more than I do."

The receptionist stared at the blue starred ribbon and bronzed medallion as I turned on my heel and headed back for the elevator doors. "Excuse me, Mr. …Weeks, was it?" she said in a voice so small that it was nearly inaudible in the voluminous chamber.

I stopped and looked back toward the gatekeeper. Her face was ashen and filled with a stoic sadness that I had seen many times on the faces of loved ones grieving their fallen heroes.

"It's Darby…Darby Weeks."

"Mr. Weeks, I lost one son in Afghanistan and another in the World Trade Center attack on September 11th. So I'll ask you this with the expectation that you will give me a straight

231

answer. Will Ms. Baines want to see you if I inform her you're here today?"

I thought for a long moment before I answered. "Honestly, I don't know."

She stared at me for a few moments without speaking. Spinning back, I pushed the down button and waited for the elevator's arrival.

"Olivia, it's Patrice," the receptionist said into the phone. "Could you please tell Ms. Baines that there is a Mr. Darby Weeks waiting in the lobby to see her. No he doesn't…I'm aware of that. Please do it anyway."

"Why did you do that?" I asked.

"You were honest, Mr. Weeks. I believe this belongs to you," she said, pointing to the medal on the counter. "You really should be more careful with what you do with it. As you know, too many have died in this awful war on terror. You apparently did something exceptional once. Make both of my sons' sacrifices mean something. Make every day of the rest of your life a gift."

My jaw began to tremble as I thought about all of the impossibilities. How had I survived? How could I live? "I'll try, Patrice."

A massive wooden door opened and Emily entered the foyer. "Hello," she said cautiously. "I'm…surprised to see you."

"Well, I'm surprised to be here so I guess we can both just stand here looking surprised."

"What are you doing here?"

"Making amends," I said, looking at Patrice, "and trying to live a meaningful life."

"Do you want to come in and talk?" Emily flashed the smallest of smiles.

232

"I'd like that, if you have the time."

"For you, Darby, I'd give an eternity."

"I just want your next forty years," I said with a wink toward Patrice as I grabbed the medal and followed Emily into belly of the corporate giant. Emily's return smile told me that she would consider it.

"I honestly didn't think I'd see you again," she said as we entered her office. It was piled high with boxes.

"Who does your decorating, U-Haul?" I asked.

"I'm in the process of packing my things. I've stepped down as the President of Tither Publishing."

"Why would you do that?"

"When I discovered that all of my success, which I thought was hard earned, had been orchestrated by that demon Pickford Marsh, I lost my desire to stay on at Tither Publishing. It's all been a lie."

"What will you do then?"

"I don't know exactly. I can literally go anywhere and do anything I want," she said with a sigh and looked out her office window. "I'm the sole heir to the Marsh family fortune and business enterprises."

"I heard you cleaned house at Aqua-Nord. You made everybody who wasn't implicated or convicted in Pickford's wrong-doings reapply for their jobs."

"My first thought was to break up and sell off Aqua-Nord in little pieces – death by a thousand cuts, but then I had an epiphany. Why not transform it into the world's true alternative energy leader? Pour billions into new research and build the largest network of wind, solar, geothermal, and fuel cell alternatives. A solar panel on every home! Imagine the possibilities?"

"I didn't think environmental issues interested you," I said.

"They don't," Emily replied, "that's why I appointed someone to lead the new Aqua-Nord, someone whose passion for the environment I knew would drive the dream of an energy independent world and make it a reality."

"Who'd you pick?"

"Finnegan Doyle."

"You're crazy," I said with a laugh. "He's bound to kill the first person who disagrees with him in a board meeting."

"Perhaps, but I also know he won't stop or let anything get in his way of achieving the goal. He's the perfect person for the job."

"Speaking of jobs, you're looking at the new head research librarian in charge of the Rauner Special Collections Library at Dartmouth College. Horatio retired and he apparently had the power to name his own successor."

"You're kidding me. Does Dartmouth know that they hired a book thief to guard their priceless collection?" she said jokingly.

"I didn't steal any book, I just borrowed a page and forgot to return it. It was a little overdue," I said defensively.

"Yeah, like thirty-seven years overdue."

"What? I returned it."

Emily laughed, touching the pearl necklace around her neck. "Well, I'm very happy for you. It sounds like you'll have your hands full managing that collection."

"Horatio said there are endless secrets and intrigue awaiting discovery in the Special Collections. He also said I would need the assistance of a shrewd College Archivist to aide in my new literary quests."

234

"Well, I'm sure you'll find the perfect person." Emily forced a smile. She lifted a wine glass from her desk, took a sip and then turned back to the window.

"I already have, that's why I'm here," I said.

She dropped her glass to the floor and looked at me with wide eyes. "I don't know anything about being a college archivist."

"Good, because I don't know anything about being a research librarian. We'll learn together as we go and read a lot of great books along the way," I said, resting Silas' red leather-bound book on her desk.

"What's this?" she asked.

"Our next adventure," I said, pulling Emily close and knowing that I would never let her go again.

THE END

ABOUT THE AUTHOR

CRAIG C. CHARLES was born in St. Louis, Missouri in 1970 and grew up in Madison, Connecticut. He graduated from Arizona State University in 1993 and went on to earn a Masters of Education degree from Keene State College in 2004. He has worked as a certified teacher in New Hampshire public schools since 2001. He lives in New Hampshire with his family. This is his debut novel.

www.craigccharles.com
Twitter: @GraniteWriter